4/85
V6

"I Just Fought a Knock-Down, Drag-Out Battle for You, Lady. I've Never Fought over a Woman in My Life."

"Max, this has gone far enough. I won't have any more violence in this house!" She backed another step, chilled at the implacable look on his face.

"No," he agreed. "No violence."

"I'll call the police!"

"Not just now." He spoke almost absently as he came to a halt a foot away and lifted a hand to touch the cheek Nick had struck. "If he ever tries to hit you again I'll kill him. You belong to me," he repeated in a soft, rasping voice. "I just won you fair and square." He pulled her into his arms.

Dear Reader:

SILHOUETTE DESIRE is an exciting new line of contemporary romances from Silhouette Books. During the past year, many Silhouette readers have written in telling us what other types of stories they'd like to read from Silhouette, and we've kept these comments and suggestions in mind in developing SILHOUETTE DESIRE.

DESIREs feature all of the elements you like to see in a romance, plus a more sensual, provocative story. So if you want to experience all the excitement, passion and joy of falling in love, then SILHOUETTE DESIRE is for you.

Karen Solem
Editor-in-Chief
Silhouette Books

STEPHANIE JAMES
Wizard

Silhouette Desire

Published by Silhouette Books New York

America's Publisher of Contemporary Romance

SILHOUETTE BOOKS
300 E. 42nd St., New York, N.Y. 10017

Copyright © 1985 by Jayne Krentz Inc.

Distributed by Pocket Books

ISBN: 0-373-05211-1

First Silhouette Books printing June, 1985

10 9 8 7 6 5 4 3 2 1

America's Publisher of Contemporary Romance

Printed in the U.S.A.

BC91

STEPHANIE JAMES

readily admits that the chief influence on her writing is her "lifelong addiction to romantic daydreaming." She has spent the last nine years living and working with her engineer husband in a wide variety of places, including the Caribbean, the Southeast and the Pacific Northwest. Ms. James currently resides in California. Stephanie James is a pseudonym for Jayne Krentz, who also writes as Jayne Castle.

Books by Stephanie James

1

She preferred cowboys.

She was like a brilliantly plumed bird who had accidentally invaded his serenely black-and-white world, bringing life and color and enthusiasm. And she preferred cowboys.

Maximilian Travers swallowed a sigh along with his wine and considered the vibrant young woman sitting across from him. Sophia Athena Bennet was making it very clear that she had no real interest in professors of mathematics, with or without tenure. She was sharing dinner with him tonight in this plush Dallas restaurant purely out of a sense of duty.

Didn't she understand that even staid professors of mathematics sometimes found themselves attracted to members of the opposite sex? Or would she care, he asked himself wryly, that something about her vivid, animated presence tugged at his awareness? Probably not. She preferred cowboys.

Max eyed her over the rim of his wine glass as she

went into a long and, he suspected, deliberately boring discussion of the staggering growth of Dallas, Texas. Even when she was trying to be dull, Sophy Bennet seemed to glow with barely repressed energy. He had never met anyone quite like her, he realized.

It wasn't that she was particularly beautiful; she wasn't. But she intrigued and tantalized him in a way he had never before experienced around a woman. She was the embodiment of warm, feminine energy, whereas he was accustomed to genteel, academic composure. She was slightly outrageous excitement, and he was used to well-bred civility.

"They're calling us the Third Coast, you know," Sophy said chattily in her low, faintly husky voice. "Lots of high-tech industry has moved in, and we've become a major financial center what with all the banking and brokerage firms. A real boomtown! Honestly, even those of us who live here have a hard time keeping track of the skyline. It changes so often." There was a subtle emphasis on "those of us who live here," and Max knew he was once again being delicately told that he did not belong. At least, not around her.

But he was getting accustomed to the not-so-subtle hints. He ignored this one in favor of studying Sophy's eyes. He really liked those eyes, he decided. A wonderful mixture of blue and green that kept a man guessing about the true color. Vivid. Everything about Sophy Bennet was vivid. Her amber brown hair was a mane of curls that fell to her shoulders in a frothy mass, framing strong, animated features. Actually, Max told himself, classical beauty would have been superfluous in Sophy's case. It would probably have detracted from the striking lines of her face. The expressive mouth, the firm angle of her nose, and the wide, slanting blue-green eyes somehow managed to be quite captivating all on their own. And they hinted at an inner strength.

The wild, scarcely controlled tangle of curls was a

dramatic style that was more than echoed in her clothes. A blouse with a peplum and huge, puffy sleeves, done in glittering shades of vermilion and turquoise, was belted over a narrow skirt of jonquil yellow and turquoise. The belt itself was a massive affair of what appeared to be stainless steel links and red leather. It wrapped Sophy's slim waist very tightly, emphasizing the slenderness of her small figure. She wore turquoise pantyhose and high-heeled, strappy little turquoise sandals. The overall effect, combined with the wide yellow bracelet cuffs she had on each wrist, was enough to make any head turn.

"Your parents will be pleased to hear you're happily settled in Dallas," he murmured into the first conversational pause. It hadn't been easy to find the pause. Sophy had kept up a running monologue on Dallas since he had arrived at her apartment earlier that evening in his rented Ford.

She gave him a repressive glance and took a large bite of her roasted bell pepper salad. "No, they won't. Dr. Travers, my parents haven't been happy with me since I was three years old, when it became obvious that I was not going to be a little child prodigy. I am now twenty-eight and they're still hoping I'm a late bloomer." Suddenly she smiled, a ravishing, brilliant smile that seemed to contain all the mischief and promise of every woman who had ever lived. "Haven't you guessed why Mom and Dad asked you to look me up here in Dallas, Dr. Travers?"

"Please, call me Max." He had the feeling he was about to be deliberately pushed off-stride, and he wasn't at all sure how to deal with the coming taunt.

The glittering smile widened with amused warmth. "They're hoping you'll fall madly in love with me, seduce and, of course, marry me. They should know better, naturally. After all, they're both certifiable geniuses themselves, so you'd think they'd know that the chances of another genius, especially a mathematical genius, falling head over heels in love with a nongenius are pretty remote. But I imagine they're still praying for some alternative to the Disaster."

"An alternative?" Max heard himself ask blankly.

"Sure. They're undoubtedly hoping for another shot at a crop of little geniuses. They never got a second chance after me, you see. Mom was told she shouldn't have any more children. They were stuck with one chance at producing a wizard to follow in their footsteps, and they wound up with me. I don't think they will ever fully accept the situation, poor dears." She sounded affectionately regretful.

"I see." Did he sound as bewildered as he felt? Max wondered.

"About the only thing I can do to salvage the situation in their eyes is marry and hope their genes will combine through me with the genes of someone like you and produce the child I should have been," Sophy explained wryly.

"But you, uh, don't intend to carry out their wishes?" he hazarded warily.

"Marry a brilliant mathematician like yourself?" she scoffed. "Hardly. I spent all of my childhood and young adult years competing against geniuses. I'll be damned if I'll turn around now that I'm free and marry someone like you! No offense," she added quickly.

"No offense," he repeated slowly, thinking that the quick remorse in her eyes appeared to be genuine. "But you just happen to prefer cowboys?"

She grinned wickedly. "One particular cowboy."

"The one you had to explain me to this afternoon?" he pressed, remembering Sophy's dismay at having to break her date with Nick Savage.

"Nick understood. I told him you were a friend of my parents who had been asked to look me up when they learned you were going to be doing some consulting work for S & J Technology. He realized there wasn't much I could do under the circumstances except entertain you for an evening. But now you and I have discharged our duty and we can go our separate ways, hmmm? How long will you be in Dallas, Max?"

"A few weeks," he replied neutrally.

Sophy tilted her head to one side, her blue-green eyes narrowing in amused perception. She fully comprehended the deliberate neutrality of his tone. She'd heard her father complain about such "consulting" trips often enough in the past. "You're going to hate every minute of it, aren't you? The theoretical mathematician compelled to lower himself to the real world of applied mathematics. Such a boring state of affairs," she teased. "But don't fret. It will soon be over and you can scurry back to your ivory tower. Have you done much consulting work in the past?"

"I get out of my ivory tower a couple of times a year."

"You mean you're pushed out by the university, which likes the prestige it gains when it occasionally lends you to industry, right?"

"I'm hardly *loaned*," he stressed mildly.

"No, of course not," Sophy chuckled. "You go for a very high price, don't you? What's the going rate now for the services of brilliant theoretical mathematicians? A thousand a day?"

"I don't get to keep the whole fee," he pointed out in a low voice.

"Will they let you keep enough of this particular consulting fee to enable you to buy some new clothes when you return to North Carolina?" she asked interestedly. Then, immediately chagrined at her audacity, she flushed in sudden embarrassment and reached for her wine. "Never mind, that was very rude of me," she mumbled into the Burgundy. "Besides, I know that styles among the academic elite don't change very frequently. Heavens, my father has an old tweed jacket he's worn for over twenty years. And my mother's wardrobe looks twenty years old, even if it isn't. I realize that you're quite suitably dressed for life on a university campus."

Lord, it was getting worse. Why hadn't she kept her mouth shut? She really hadn't intended to embarrass her parents' distinguished colleague, Dr. Maximilian Travers. She had set out with every intention of doing her duty tonight, even though she was well aware that both she and Max had been coerced into the untenable situation.

For just a moment she allowed herself to admit privately that under other circumstances this date wouldn't have been such a chore at all. Sophy knew she had been strangely, vitally aware of Max the moment he had entered her office to introduce himself. She had looked up from her typewriter and realized she was actually holding her breath as he approached her desk.

Then, of course, he had introduced himself and ruined everything. Yes, she should have kept her mouth shut.

"I will admit that we do tend to dress a bit more conservatively back in North Carolina," Max allowed politely. He slanted a meaningful glance around the elegant restaurant. Several of the other men were wearing obviously expensive jackets, many cut with a decidedly western flair. There was more than one pair of masculine feet clad in beautifully etched leather boots. A certain good-natured extravagance marked the attire of most people in the room, making Max's tweed jacket and white shirt seem very quiet in comparison.

It wasn't just the plain white shirt, the too-narrow tie and the old tweed jacket that marked him, Sophy thought to herself. It was also the horn-rimmed glasses that framed his serious, smoky eyes and the plastic pack of pens and pencils in his left pocket. A "nerd pack" as it was amusingly called by her co-workers at S & J Technology. Such packs were carried by engineers and mathematicians the world over and had become a symbol of their dedication to numbers. Sophy shuddered delicately. She hated numbers. Hated math of any kind.

But even if Max Travers had not arrived equipped with the accoutrements of a typical mathematician cum university professor, she would have recognized him anywhere. After all, she had spent her formative years surrounded by his type.

Perhaps it was the intense, undeniable intelligence that flared in those smoke-colored eyes that identified him. Or it might have been the quiet, analytical air that was so much a part of him. Sophy had the feeling that Max Travers never did anything on impulse. He would carefully weigh all options, analyze all data and catalog every scrap of information before acting. He looked out of place here in this flashy restaurant, and he certainly looked out of place as her date. Max should have been sipping sherry at a faculty party and discussing his latest treatise on math with someone who could understand.

Too bad he had that faintly disapproving, wet-blanket attitude, Sophy found herself thinking. Too bad he was brilliant. Too bad he was from that other world, which she had avoided so carefully for the past few years. Too bad about a lot of things because there had been that breathless moment just before he had introduced himself. It was a moment that existed only in her imagination, she sternly told herself.

But all the same Sophy found herself wondering what it would be like to see passion in that remote, smoky gaze. Instantly she stifled the dangerous question. She had to admit, however, that there was something about the fiercely carved masculine features that subtly invited her awareness. Almost absently Sophy pegged his age at thirty-five or thirty-six. For a man who had spent his entire life in the rarefied atmosphere of academia, he didn't appear soft or weak. But then, who knew better than she that there was nothing particularly soft about genius?

Maximilian Travers wasn't conventionally attractive. The austere line of his nose and the aggressive planes of cheek and jaw left little room for good looks. Instead his features revealed an inner power that wasn't diminished even by the severe white shirt, old-fashioned tie and well-worn jacket. Sophy decided she didn't care for the implication of masculine strength. Oh, she liked strong men well enough; she just didn't like strength allied to brilliance. It didn't seem fair.

It would have been reassuring to discover a paunch beneath the old jacket, but there was none. The narrow, scuffed leather belt Max wore clasped a lean waist, and Sophy had to admit that she had seen no other signs of physical weakness in him either. Very unfair, really.

"Your parents said you just recently moved to Dallas?"

"That's right. A few months ago," Sophy agreed easily as she buttered a chunk of French bread. "It took me a while to find a new job. I'm afraid Mom and Dad are still shuddering over the one I did find." She lowered the butter knife and leaned forward melodramatically. "I'm only a secretary, you know," she confided in a stage whisper. "The horror of it all. A Bennet working as a mere secretary." Then she sat back and smiled blandly. "But it's better than selling clothes in a department store, which is what I was doing in Los Angeles, don't you think?"

"I wouldn't know," Max mumbled a bit uneasily.

Sophy's smile broadened. "Of course you wouldn't. I'll bet you've never had to do anything so mundane in your whole life, have you? Shall I take a stab at outlining your past?"

"You don't know me at all," he protested quietly.

"The hell I don't." She grinned. "I know your kind. How's this? Declared academically gifted at an early age, perhaps even before first grade. Immediately placed in advanced preschools, advanced kindergarten and then into classes for the mentally gifted. Probably skipped a couple of grades here and there. Finished high school a few years ahead of the rest of the plodders and entered college at a tender age. Zipped through college and went directly into a doctoral program. From there it was merely a hop, skip and a jump to the faculty of a fine university where your talents are appreciated and duly rewarded with a corner office and a light teaching load. Right so far?"

"Do you read tea leaves as a hobby?" There was a dry note to his voice, and his smoky eyes narrowed fractionally. It occurred to Sophy that there might be more than academic temperament buried in this man. There might be genuine male temper. And that implied passion. Sophy brushed the thought aside. Mathematicians were rarely passionate about anything except math.

"No tea leaves," she responded airily. "It's just that, as I said, I know your kind. I spent too many years desperately trying to keep up with your type and failing. I'm lucky I wasn't traumatized for life. Or perhaps I was," she added thoughtfully. She reached for her wine glass and smiled again.

"You don't appear terribly traumatized."

"Just ask my parents. They think I'm on the verge of going off the deep end. Twenty-eight years old and still changing jobs regularly. And what terrible jobs! Cocktail waitress, department store clerk, secretary. So demeaning for someone who should have inherited brains." Sophy shuddered delicately.

"You don't appear any more demeaned than you do traumatized." Max paused while the waiter served the entrée, lamb with apricot sauce.

"Well, to tell you the truth," Sophy confided cheerfully, "I really don't suffer from either of those two conditions. Not anymore. Not since I discovered the real world. I do very well in the real world, Max."

"What did you mean, you spent a lot of years trying to keep up with 'my kind'?" Max frowned down at his lamb chop. He was accustomed to mint sauce, not apricot sauce, on lamb. Sophy had recommended the apricot but now he wasn't so sure.

"I'm afraid my parents were never reconciled to the fact that they had produced an ordinary little girl, not a brilliant little prodigy," Sophy explained equably. "It was very hard on them. Go ahead. Try the apricot sauce. It's delicious on lamb. Live a little, Max." She ignored his frown. "Where was I? Oh, yes. As I said, my not being brilliant was hard on my parents. They had been so sure that the mating of two highly intelligent people would produce intelligent offspring. They refused to believe otherwise and, of course, no one dared to tell them differently."

Max looked up, still frowning. "What do you mean?"

"Well, before he went into semiretirement, Dad was one of the leading mathematicians in the country—"

"He still is," Max interrupted.

"Yes, I know, but in those days he was wildly sought after by just about every university in the nation. They all wanted him as a shining ornament for their math departments. The last thing anyone wanted to do was risk offending him. My mother, being such a prominent physicist, was also considered a prize. The pair of them wrote their own tickets as far as their careers were concerned. Naturally I was pushed into advanced, avant-garde classes, the kind they have on campuses for the children of the faculty. Everyone knew who I

16

was and none of the teachers wanted the responsibility of informing my parents that I wasn't exactly a genius. Mom and Dad kept thinking that I was just late in developing my talent, whatever it was." She leaned forward expectantly. "How's the lamb?"

"It's all right," Max allowed cautiously.

She sat back, smiling. "Of course it is. Geniuses tend to be much too unadventurous. Back to my traumatic childhood. Well, Mom and Dad kept shoving me into the most advanced classes they could find. Classrooms that were filled with little boys and girls who, like you, really did grow up to be geniuses. I consider my school years the worst years of my life."

"Because you always found yourself competing with people like me?"

"Exactly. Oh, I had my role in the grand scheme of things, I suppose. I mean, with me around, the rest of you always looked positively brilliant. I helped maintain the class curve, as it were. The low end of the curve was my slot. The *very* low end. Do you have any idea what it was like to always be the dumbest kid in class?" Sophy shook her head once, answering her own question. The mane of amber curls bounced in a lively manner and her eyes brimmed with laughter. "No, of course you don't. What a silly question. You were always the one bringing up the class average to levels that were impossible for people like me to even approach."

"Did you drop out of school?"

"Oh, no, I stuck it out through high school, and, although my grades were terrible, my father managed to convince a small college in the Midwest to accept me. College, I discovered, wasn't really bad at all. It was chock-full of real people, not just you gifted types. I held my own very nicely in college, but I was so soured on formal education by that time that I still disliked the work. To please my parents, though, I made it to

17

graduation. Then I pronounced myself free, informed Mom and Dad that there was no help for it, I was doomed to be average, and went out to make my way in the world. It's a world they know very little about, however, so they worry constantly. They would feel far more content if I would just get married to a proper math wiz such as yourself and settle down to producing a bunch of little wizards."

"Something you have no intention of doing?" Max eyed her questioningly.

"Not on your Ph.D.! Don't worry, Dr. Travers," Sophy chuckled, "you're safe. I guarantee I have absolutely no matrimonial designs on your person."

"Only on the person of a certain cowboy?"

"Nick's not just any cowboy," Sophy drawled. "He's an ex-rodeo star with a sizable ranch outside of Dallas."

"Are you going to marry him?" Max persisted.

"We're considering the matter," she allowed loftily. "Nick and I lead very full lives and we're content to let our relationship develop naturally."

"And after things develop *naturally,* will you settle down and raise lots of little cowboys? I should think Texas already had enough of those," Max commented with a hint of irritation.

"Spoken with the true disdain of the intellectual elite for the rest of us lowly mortals," she shot back, some of her amusement fading.

To her surprise, Max had the grace to redden slightly. "Sophy, I didn't mean to sound elitist about it."

"No, I expect it comes naturally. Don't worry, Max, I understand. Far better than you will ever know. When you go back to North Carolina, feel free to tell my parents that I am alive and thriving in Dallas and that I have no intention of becoming a broodmare for geniuses."

"I think you misunderstood their motives in asking me to look you up," Max said repressively.

"Dr. Travers," Sophy countered with rueful humor, "I may not understand differential equations or vector analysis, but I do understand my mother and father. Furthermore, I think it's safe to say that I understand people in general a good deal better than Mom and Dad and you ever will."

"Sophy," Max began in a severely pedantic tone, "when your parents learned that I was being sent to S & J Technology for a consulting trip, it was quite reasonable that they should ask me to introduce myself to their daughter. There was no ulterior motive."

Sophy shook her head. "Take it from me," she said with a grin. "There was. You've been tagged as good breeding stock, as we say here in Texas. They'd be absolutely thrilled if you got me pregnant."

"Sophy, I think you're being deliberately outrageous." The high bones of Max's cheeks were stained a dull red beneath the natural tan of his skin.

"We underachievers sometimes resort to such tactics to hold our own against people like you," Sophy admitted pleasantly. "But in this case, I'm only trying to give you fair warning. Not that you're in any genuine danger."

"Because you prefer cowboys," he concluded flatly.

"I prefer just about anyone to a genius. And if you're honest, you'll admit that you would be horrified at the idea of being tied to someone who wasn't as intelligent as yourself. No one likes to be mismatched. It's extraordinarily painful, believe me."

"People like me intimidate you?" he asked quietly.

"Not anymore! But your type did a hell of a good job of it all during my school years. It wasn't your fault. I was the misfit sparrow thrust in among the mental peacocks."

Max suddenly, unexpectedly, smiled. "I would have said it was just the opposite."

"What?" Sophy eyed him uncertainly.

"I would have said you were the peacock tossed in with us rather dull sparrows," he explained gently.

Sophy blinked, taken aback at the quiet sureness of his words. Hastily she recovered. "Well, that's all over now. I'm free and I intend to remain free. As much as I love my parents, I'm not going to live my life for them. They will just have to accept the Disaster."

"When did you start calling yourself their Disaster?" he queried.

"So long ago I can't even remember. I realized very early in life that I wasn't going to be the daughter they had dreamed of producing. I'll bet your parents were absolutely delighted with you, though, weren't they?" she asked.

He glanced down at his plate as if doing a quick mathematical analysis of the position of the lamb in relation to the peas. "They seem satisfied, yes."

"Where do they live?"

"In California. They're both retired now."

Sophy sensed the shutters coming down and wondered why. Instinctively she pressed a bit further, finding herself suddenly very curious about Dr. Maximilian Travers. "Are they both from the academic world?"

"Yes."

"Mathematicians?"

"My father is a mathematician. My mother is a biologist. They were both on the faculty of a West Coast university until they elected to retire a couple of years ago."

There was a stilted inflection in his words, but Sophy couldn't quite put her finger on what was wrong. Oh, well, she told herself firmly, it wasn't her problem. Geniuses didn't need someone ordinary like herself worrying about them. "Well, I'm sure they're very pleased at your success," she said bracingly. "Have they urged you to marry and carry on the tradition of academic excellence?"

"They, uh, mention marriage occasionally. I imagine they'd like a grandchild."

"Sound just like my parents." Sophy nodded wisely.

"Sophy, it's considered natural for parents to want grandchildren."

"Ah, but in our case they wouldn't want just any sort of grandchildren, would they? They'd want little wizards. Are you going to have dessert? They make a fabulous margarita pie here."

"That sounds awful." He looked genuinely appalled.

"Be daring. After all, you'll have to go back to your ivory tower in a couple of weeks, and you may never get another chance to sample margarita pie."

"I don't know. Maybe a slice of cheesecake. . . ."

But Sophy was already signaling the waiter. There was something amusingly pleasant about pushing a wizard around a bit, even if it was only over something as trivial as margarita pie. "We'll have two margarita pies," she announced as the waiter hurried over to their table.

The man swept off with the order before Max could change it. Accepting the failure with good grace, he gave Sophy a rather hard smile. "It will be an experience, I suppose."

"You'll love it, Max. Where are you staying while you're in Dallas?"

"One of the downtown hotels." He told her the name and she raised her expressive brows.

"My, my. Nothing but the best for visiting genius mathematicians, hmmm? That's a very posh place."

"Perhaps you'd like to drop by for an afterdinner drink in the lounge before I take you home?" he suggested politely.

"Oh, I don't think so, thank you. It's getting rather

late and I'm sure you've got better things to do than
entertain your colleagues' daughter. Besides, I told Nick
I'd meet him for a drink around ten. He's spending the
evening with some fellow ranchers at one of the local
clubs. When I told him I wasn't going to be free tonight,
he decided to join his friends for a few hours and wait
for me."

Max abruptly became aware that his fingers were
curling very tightly around his knife as he set it down
beside his plate. She'd set up another date for the
evening. After she left him, Sophia Athena Bennet was
planning on going straight to another man. The knowledge was strangely annoying.

"Your cowboy didn't mind your coming out with me
this evening?" he asked deliberately as he finished the
lamb and waited in resignation for the margarita pie.

"Oh, he wasn't thrilled, but he understood. After all,
he's got family, too, and he knows they can make
demands."

"It's not your family that made the demand, it was
me," Max felt obliged to point out in a very even tone.

"Only because my family asked you to look me up."

"It doesn't occur to you that I might have wanted to
have dinner with you?"

"In a word, no," she said, grinning.

He winced inwardly because in a sense she was
absolutely right. He *had* looked her up as a favor to her
parents. But the moment he'd seen her, he'd been
grateful he'd had the excuse of knowing Paul and Anna
Bennet. Without that he wouldn't have been at all
certain how to approach such an alien creature. In the
natural order of things, he simply didn't encounter
women like Sophy very often. Dealing with her was
going to be like dealing with a new and exotic math
frontier.

"Sophy . . ."

"Oh, I realize you might be a bit lonely here in

Dallas," she said quickly. "Maybe having dinner with me was better than sitting alone in a hotel room."

"It was," he agreed dryly.

"But not much, hmmm? You're probably bored already. We haven't even touched on the theory of relativity or Boolean logic."

"Believe it or not, I do find other things in life interesting besides mathematics!" he growled.

"I'm sure you do," she soothed in a condescending tone that irritated him even further. "But I don't know any more about those things than I do about math, so I'd make pretty poor company."

"I wasn't talking about academic interests," Max gritted as the margarita pie arrived. He eyed the dessert apprehensively.

"Really? What other things were you referring to, then?" Sophy asked idly, digging into her pie with obvious relish.

He seriously considered telling her that professors of mathematics were just as capable as anyone else of being interested in sex, but almost immediately dismissed the idea. If he said anything that blunt, she'd probably fling the pie in his face and get up on the table to declare once and for all that she was not a broodmare for wizards. Seeing no acceptable alternative and mindful, as always, of his role as a gentleman and a scholar, Max shook his head. "Never mind. Where is your cowboy going to meet you? Should I drop you somewhere downtown?"

"No, you can take me home. He'll be meeting me there."

"I see. Will he be staying the night?" What the hell had made him ask that? Max wondered savagely.

Instantly the mischievous smile in her eyes disappeared. "That's really none of your business, is it, Dr. Travers?"

He was learning, Max thought. When she called him

Dr. Travers, she was annoyed. "No," he admitted, "it isn't. I'm sorry I asked."

The smile reappeared. "I'm sure my parents are just as curious."

"Have they met him?"

"No," Sophy said carelessly. "How's the pie?"

"Not nearly as bad as I had feared."

"You shouldn't be so shy about new experiences, Max."

"In your own way, you can be quite condescending, did you know that?" he asked coolly.

She chuckled. "This is turning into a pretty horrible evening, isn't it? Sorry about that, but I could have warned you. People like you and me don't mix very well together. Don't fret about it. You've done your duty and you can report back to my parents that you did, indeed, look me up while you were in Dallas. That's all they can reasonably ask of you."

"Meaning they won't demand that I perform stud services, too?" The words were out before he could stop them, and Max was shocked at his lack of control. What the hell was the matter with him? He never talked like this! Especially not to women. It was all wrapped up with the fact that Sophy was going straight home to that damned cowboy.

"I think you can rest assured that they won't embarrass everyone concerned by asking whether or not you managed to sleep with me while you were here in Dallas," she shot back. "Now if you don't mind, Max, I would like to leave. Nick will be expecting me."

Max nodded, not trusting himself to speak for a few seconds while he recovered his equilibrium. Mutely he pulled out his worn leather wallet and found his credit card. Then he signed the slip the waiter had prepared. He was getting up from the table, his mind on taking Sophy home to her cowboy, when she abruptly put a restraining hand on his arm and smiled pointedly.

"You forgot your copy of the credit slip."

"What? Oh." Unaccountably embarrassed at the small oversight, Max hastily reached out to tear off the slip.

"Don't worry, my father does that all the time. So does Mom, for that matter."

Max winced at the unspoken implications concerning absentminded professors. He had the sinking feeling the cowboy never had such lapses.

"Are you sure you don't want to stop by my hotel for a nightcap?" It was a halfhearted attempt that Max knew was doomed to failure. He had always been a little socially awkward simply because socializing had seemed relatively unimportant in the grand scheme of his life. But tonight he would have given a lot for some suave social polish. Tonight it would have been very pleasant to be the kind of man capable of sweeping a woman like Sophy off her feet.

"No, thanks," Sophy said predictably as she slipped into the front seat of the rented Ford. "It's almost ten."

"And you wouldn't want to keep the cowboy waiting, would you?" Max muttered under his breath as she shut the door. He wasn't sure whether or not she had heard him. If she had, she chose to ignore the hint of masculine disgust. Or worse, perhaps she found it amusing.

The drive into the north side of Dallas was accompanied by another running monologue on the city's growth and prospects. At several points along the way Max was sorely tempted to clamp a hand over Sophia Athena Bennet's sweet mouth to halt the flow of deliberately boring words.

And then what? Stop the car and drag her into the back seat? Hardly the sort of behavior expected of a tenured professor of mathematics. Also hardly the sort of behavior he was accustomed to indulging in around women. Max realized with a start of surprise that he'd never met a woman he wanted to treat in such an elementary fashion. Christ! If her father only knew what he was thinking at the moment. Dr. Paul Bennet was a gentleman and a scholar and assumed that Max was in the same league.

"Well, Max, thank you very much for dinner." Sophy sounded relieved as the Ford pulled into the driveway of her garden apartment complex. "I suppose I'll see you around the office off and on for the next few weeks."

"You don't sound terribly thrilled at the prospect."

Instantly an expression of genuine contrition swept over her face, and she lightly patted his arm with five carmine-tipped nails. In the shadowed interior of the car, her eyes seemed very wide and deep.

"I'm sorry if I've offended you, Max. Please believe me, I didn't intend to. I know this evening was just a duty date for both of us. But now we've met our obligations, so there's no need to worry about the matter further. You can go back to North Carolina in a few weeks and assure my parents I'm alive and well out here. I'm going to be seeing them myself weekend after next when I go back to Chapel Hill for an award ceremony honoring Mom. I'll give you some good press when I see them. We'll both be off the hook."

She was already sliding along the seat, her hand leaving his arm as she opened the car door. A sudden glare of headlights in the rearview mirror caught Max's attention, and he turned to glance out the back window in time to see a long white Lincoln purring to a halt behind the Ford.

The cowboy had arrived to claim his lady. As Max watched the vivid creature he had just taken to dinner fly into the arms of the tall man with the Stetson who had just alighted from the depths of the Lincoln, he felt a wave of grim resentment.

It was a resentment that had no logical basis, he told himself roughly, and put the Ford in gear.

No logical basis unless you counted the very primitive logic that Max wanted to be the man who spent the night in Sophia Athena's bed.

Damned cowboy.

2

~∞∞∞∞∞∞∞~

She had told Max Travers that her relationship with Nick Savage was developing naturally, and Sophy was positive that was true. Even as she hurried from the Ford to meet Nick, Sophy told herself that it was a great relief to end the evening with Max.

But the relief she experienced was not precisely the right sort, she realized vaguely. She ought to feel as though she had just escaped a dull, boring evening with a man in whom she could never be even remotely interested, even as a friend.

Instead the feeling welling up inside was one of relief at having escaped a potentially dangerous situation. And there was absolutely no reason for the sensation. Deliberately she pushed the thought out of her mind as she lifted her face for Nick's kiss. Tall and rugged, with black, wavy hair and bedroom eyes, Nick Savage was the perfect antidote to an evening spent with a wizard.

"What are you smilin' at, darlin'?" Nick asked as he took her hand and walked toward the apartment door.

Sophy told herself that his Texas drawl was sensual and sexy. She wasn't about to admit that occasionally it got on her nerves. The good-ole-boy twang was as much a part of Nick as his Lincoln, she reminded herself.

"I was thinking how good an ex–rodeo cowboy looks after an evening spent with a professor of math," Sophy teased, digging her key out of the tiny leather purse that was clipped to her wide belt. "Honestly, Nick, I thought the evening would never end."

"I can't say I'm sorry to hear your visitin' genius was a little dull." Nick took the key from her hand and used it on the front door. "Just don't expect me to give up any more evenings so that you can do your duty," he warned as he stepped into the hall behind her.

"Never again." With a happy sigh, Sophy turned and put her arms around his neck, standing on tiptoe to kiss him.

Nick wrapped one arm around her waist and used his free hand to remove the gray Stetson. With practiced skill he sent it sailing across the room to land on the coffee table. There it struck a pile of magazines and sent them slithering to the floor.

"You're getting awfully good at that," Sophy marveled, ignoring her scattered magazines.

"I intend to get a whole lot better, darlin'. Pretty soon I'm gonna make that hat land on the bedpost in your bedroom."

His meaning was clear and Sophy didn't demur. Surely it was only a matter of time before she went to bed with Nick Savage. After all, they were falling in love and they were both mature adults. If the truth were known, Sophy had already wondered silently at Nick's willingness to be put off this long. But he seemed to respect her desire to be sure of their emotions. It was one of the many things she liked about him.

The only thing that secretly bothered her on occasion was why she, herself, kept hesitating.

"I'll get the brandy," Sophy said after a moment, slipping from his arms to head for the kitchen. "I don't know about you, but I need something."

"Don't mind if I do a little celebratin' myself. Won a fair piece of change off Cal Henderson this evening."

"So that's what you spent the evening doing— playing poker. Shame on you." She sent him a laughingly reproachful glance across the counter that divided the living room from the sleek, modern kitchen.

"Honey, any Texan worth his salt plays poker on occasion. Be downright suspiciously unpatriotic and unneighborly to refuse a friendly game." With a satisfied grin, Nick threw himself down onto the melon-colored sofa and propped his booted feet on the Lucite coffee table.

Sophy smiled at the sight of him sprawled in her living room. Nick Savage was everything that had traditionally attracted women to cowboys. He had a handsome, suntanned face that was attractively open and rugged, and he was over six feet tall. He had the casual western manners that thrived in Texas, and he wore the local style of clothing well. The feet on her coffee table were encased in hand-tooled gray leather, and the gray, western-cut suit he wore was perfectly detailed from the yoked shoulders to the flare-legged pants.

As usual, Nick wore the huge, inlaid-silver belt buckle that proclaimed his past championship status as a rodeo star. It was a trifle unfortunate that a small paunch was beginning to appear over the edge of the buckle, but there was still enough masculine, western-style arrogance about him to pique any woman's interest. Sophy felt quite lucky that he had taken to her at the party where they met.

Cradling a brandy glass in each palm, she walked out of the starkly done black-and-white kitchen and into the colorful living room. Sophy's love of exotic, eye-catching hues was evident not only in her apparel but throughout her home.

The melon-colored couch on which Nick lounged was set off by vanilla walls and a jade green carpet. The rainbow-hued easy chair by the fireplace had a mate on the opposite side of the room, and here and there dramatic touches of black underscored the vivid effect. It was a room that fit her personality and her lifestyle.

"Ah missed you this evenin', darlin'." Nick draped a casual arm around Sophy's shoulders as she sank down beside him and curled her feet under her. He smiled, fingering one of the huge sleeves of the blouse she wore. "This new?"

"Umm." Sophy swallowed a sip of brandy. "Just finished it yesterday. Like it?"

"Oh, I like it well enough. Just don't fancy you wearin' it for the first time with that visitin' nerd." Nick moved his fingers absently on her shoulder.

For some reason his use of the term "nerd" to describe Max bothered Sophy, although she admitted she might easily have used it herself. With a touch of restlessness, she put down her brandy glass and sat forward to restack the magazines that had been pushed onto the rug by the flying Stetson.

"You sure do subscribe to a lot of those business magazines," Nick observed, watching her idly.

"A woman who has plans to start her own business has to do a lot of groundwork." Sophy smiled, piling a government pamphlet profiling successful entrepreneurial women on top of a magazine describing women in business.

"All your plans still goin' along fine?"

"Oh, yes. In a few more months I should have the financial backing I need."

"Won't be no need for my woman to work, you know," Nick said softly.

Sophy ignored the comment about not needing to work and told herself that the possessive sound of "my woman" was very nice to hear. She gracefully yielded the brandy glass when he reached out to remove it from her hand, and then she allowed herself to be drawn close.

Nick's kiss was warm and pleasurable, his mouth moving on hers with undeniable expertise. Sophy gave herself up to it, wondering what it would be like when she and Nick finally went to bed together. Soon. The time would soon arrive. Nick had been so considerate, so patient, so respectful of her desire to be certain. . . .

"I wish to hell I didn't have to get up at five tomorrow mornin'," Nick groaned a few minutes later.

"That trip to Phoenix?"

"Yeah. You'll be a good girl while I'm gone?" Nick nuzzled her neck.

"Of course."

"You'd better." He got reluctantly to his feet, collecting the Stetson. "Much as I hate to leave, I reckon I'll have to get goin'. Long drive back out to the ranch."

"When will you be back?" Sophy asked conversationally as she walked beside him to the Lincoln. There was very little of the long, white luxury automobile that wasn't decorated with chrome. The license plate was personalized with the brand of Nick's ranch, the Diamond S.

"Wednesday," Nick said as he stopped beside the car to light one of his long, dark cigarettes. He cupped his palm around the flame from the gold lighter, which was also embossed with a diamond and an S, and bent his head to light the cigarette. It was a delightfully masculine gesture that made Sophy smile. Too bad she didn't approve of smoking, she thought. It could be so damn sexy. She'd bet her new electronic sewing machine that Max Travers had never touched a cigarette in his life. He would have decided long ago that it was foolish to take the health risk.

"I'll be back in time to take you to the Everet shindig," Nick went on as he exhaled. He wrapped his arm around her shoulders and leaned back against the car.

"I'm looking forward to it. A real Texas barbecue, hmmm?"

"They pull out all the stops once a year. We'll have a good time. Bring your swimsuit. There's a pool that folks will be using." He took the cigarette out of his mouth and bent his head to kiss her goodbye.

Sophy steadfastly ignored the taste of smoke in his mouth, but she couldn't quite ignore the sudden jab of pain in her midsection.

"Ummph!"

"What's wrong, honey?"

"Nothing," she assured him quickly, adjusting her position. "I just came close to committing hari-kari on your belt buckle."

He chuckled, glancing down at the huge silver championship buckle with evident satisfaction. "A good year. Had some wild times on the circuit."

"Miss the rodeo?"

He shrugged. "It's a young man's game. Best to get out while you're on top. And after Dad died, the ranch needed attention, anyway. It's time I settled down." He smiled meaningfully. "With the right woman."

Sophy smiled up at him brilliantly and stood on tiptoe to brush his mouth with her own. "Good night, Nick. Drive carefully."

"I will. I'll call you on Wednesday when I get back from Phoenix."

Sophy stood in her doorway for a minute after Nick left, watching the big white barge of a car slip silently down the street and out of sight. At least she'd managed to spend a little time with Nick tonight. The duty date hadn't spoiled the entire evening.

Back inside, she shook her head wryly as she began to undress for bed. If ever there were two men who were diametrical opposites, they were Nick Savage and Max Travers. One was exciting, the other quite dull. One was unintimidating intellectually; the other came from another world, the totally intimidating world of higher math. Nick would surely be a sexy, experienced lover. Max probably made love by the numbers. One would make a dynamic, successful husband, and the other would probably spend hours at a time so wrapped up in his math that he would forget he was married altogether. Sophy knew which man was right for her.

Didn't she?

"Getting married isn't like buying a bull," she advised herself as she climbed into bed wearing the plum-colored nightgown she had made the previous week. "I'm not looking for good breeding stock! I'm looking for love and passion and compatibility."

Tongue absently touching her lower lip, Sophy found herself wondering what would have happened if she'd accepted Max's offer of a drink at his hotel. Nothing, probably. Men like Max didn't lower themselves to making passes at women. Men like Max were gentlemen and scholars.

But if he had made a pass, attempted to take her in his arms, how would she have reacted? Why was she even asking herself the question? It was ridiculous! Annoyed, Sophy twisted onto her side and fluffed her pillow. Perhaps there had been too much tequila in that margarita pie. Something was making her imagination take some bizarre turns tonight!

She smiled wryly to herself in the darkness. Her parents would be disappointed that she and Max hadn't instantly fallen for each other. But they'd had twenty-eight years to adjust to the continuing disappointment of their only child. They'd handle this current matchmaking failure just as they'd handled all the other failures: with stoic bravery.

Deep down, in their own way, Sophy knew, they loved her, just as she loved them; but communication between parents and child had always been difficult. When she was younger, Sophy had felt as badly about the Disaster as Paul and Anna had. Guilt over her own lack of genius had kept her doggedly plodding her way through all those endless accelerated classes designed for the intellectually gifted.

As one despairing teacher after another had failed to find the courage to tell the Bennets that their daughter simply was not a genius, Sophy had begun to hate the role into which she had been cast.

"She simply doesn't apply herself," her fourth-grade teacher had explained to the Bennets at a conference. "I'm sure she has the ability, but she seems perpetually bored in class. It's like that sometimes with the truly gifted. It's hard to engage their attention, even in advanced classes such as this one, because they're so far ahead mentally."

"She'll come into her own in high school," the seventh-grade instructor had assured the Bennets. "In the meantime, all we can do is keep exposing her to as much intellectual stimulation as possible."

"She'll blossom in college," the high school teachers had insisted. "Some bright teenagers simply don't do well in high school, even in these academically accelerated classes."

And all along, the only one who had admitted the truth was Sophy. She wasn't bored in class; she was usually totally lost, desperately trying to comprehend what her fellow students picked up so easily. She wasn't failing to apply herself. She worked hard, driven by guilt and the fear of disappointing her parents.

But always there had been the wizards surrounding

her. From the day she had been sent off to the carefully selected preschool for precocious children, Sophy had been trapped in the midst of the truly brilliant.

Sophy's only satisfaction during those formative years had been pursuits that involved color and fabric. In kindergarten she had latched on to the discovery of crayons with a vengeance, going through one coloring book after another until she was designing her own coloring books. Unfortunately, the rest of the class was working on the rudiments of mathematical set theory.

In grade school, art had been taught in the accelerated classes, usually in relation to mathematical perspective and the properties of light. Sophy hadn't been overly interested in the scientific side of the matter, but she'd happily played with the watercolor paints until they were gently but firmly taken from her.

Her parents had briefly considered the possibility that her true genius might lie in the realm of art, but when she showed no great interest in drawing anything other than doll clothes, they abandoned the idea.

When she discovered dressmaking, Paul and Anna Bennet steadfastly decided to treat it as a hobby. They were still treating it that way. In all honesty, they weren't the only ones who looked on her skills as a hobby. There were times when she suspected that Nick Savage did, too. That realization was vaguely annoying, but she told herself that in time he would realize how important her budding career as a designer was to her. Firmly she dismissed the concern. Nick would learn.

Someone like Max Travers would probably never understand, though. His academic elitism would always get in the way. Not that it mattered. She could care less what Max Travers thought of her future career. But why had she felt so wary around the man tonight? Hadn't she left those old feelings of intimidation behind for good? Of course she had. So why that primitive wariness? Why had she practically run from his car tonight? It made no sense.

Sophy had put the restless questions out of her head by the next morning when she walked into the downtown high-rise building that housed S & J Technology. She had a large box under one arm, and as soon as she stepped off the elevator on the fifteenth floor and into the section where most of the clerks and secretaries worked, a murmur of anticipation went up from the group standing around the coffee machine. A half dozen people came hurrying across the room.

"Is it finished?" Marcie Fremont, who had joined the staff shortly before Sophy and who had the desk next to hers, glanced expectantly at the box.

Sophy smiled at her and began unwrapping it. Marcie had paid well for what was inside, but Sophy was satisfied that she had delivered a dress worth the money.

Co-workers privately thought the two women offered an interesting contrast. Where Sophy was vivid and colorful and slightly outrageous at times, Marcie was cool and sophisticated. Her blond hair was always confined in a sleek, businesslike twist, and her beautiful, patrician features were always made up in subdued, refined tones.

Marcie Fremont dressed for success, as she herself put it, firmly convinced that the route out of the secretarial pool was going to be easier in the right clothes. Slim, tailored suits, silk blouses and restrained jewelry comprised her professional wardrobe. The overall effect was poised, efficient and rather distant. Sophy had kept that image in mind when she'd designed the after-hours dress.

"Remember, if you don't like it, you don't have to pay for it." Sophy smiled as she lifted the lid. Marcie smiled back quickly and Sophy was pleased to see the genuine anticipation in her eyes. Lately she had sensed a kind of quiet desperation about her new friend. Secretarial work was strictly a temporary situation for Sophy, but for Marcie it could prove to be a dead end.

"If Marcie doesn't want it, I'll take it, sight unseen," Karen Gibson announced. The others standing around nearby agreed.

"I'm sure I'll like it," Marcie said firmly. The gown came fluidly out of the box to murmured gasps of appreciation. A long, body-hugging line of black crepe with the dramatic impact of a swirling white organdy collar, it was obviously perfect for Marcie Fremont. It dipped low in the back to reveal an elegant length of spine, and it was slit up one side to the knee.

Marcie reached for it with real delight. "It's stunning, Sophy. Absolutely stunning! You're a genius." She held it to her while everyone else admired the effect.

"No doubt about it," Karen remarked, "it's absolutely right for you, Marcie."

The outer door opened at that moment and everyone swung around to see Max Travers standing just inside the room. There was a faint frown of curiosity on his face. He took in the sight of the women grouped around the sleek black gown and looked as if he were about to back out of the room. He held a sheaf of papers clutched in one hand as his eyes sought out Sophy.

Look at her, he thought as he found her instantly, so full of warmth and life and enthusiasm. She'd make any man happy. Any man who could hold her, that was. And she only let cowboys hold her. Damn it to hell, what's the matter with me? Grimly he took a grip on himself, unaware that his frown had intensified.

"Excuse me," Max began aloofly. "I was told I could get someone down here to type up these notes for me."

Feeling mildly chagrined at having been the one to create the decidedly unbusinesslike scene, Sophy stepped forward. "I'll take those, Dr. Travers."

Max's smoky eyes darkened behind the horn-rimmed glasses as he thrust the papers into her hand with an abrupt gesture. "What's all the fuss about over that dress?" he asked gruffly, nodding his head at the small group still hovering over the black gown.

"I just finished designing it for Marcie." Absently Sophy flipped through the sheaf of papers.

"Oh." Max glanced at the dress with more curiosity. "I didn't know you sewed."

"My parents have tried to keep it a deep, dark secret. We all pretend it's just a hobby." She nodded at the papers. "Anything unusual about these notes? Want them done in a standard format?"

Max brought his attention back to the papers. "It's company proprietary stuff, so don't make any copies. Your management probably would just as soon not have any duplicates floating around."

"Max, you can trust everyone here." Sophy smiled blandly. "We all work for the company. We wouldn't spill its little secrets. Besides, who here could understand all this complicated stuff about a mathematical model for a chemical processing system?"

Max cocked an eyebrow. "You apparently understand it enough to tell what it is just by glancing through a few notes."

Sophy shook her head indulgently. "I have a good mathematical and scientific vocabulary, thanks to all those years spend among wizards. I can translate what you're saying, but that doesn't mean I can comprehend it. It's like being a medical secretary. She might have the vocabulary for writing up the doctor's notes, but she couldn't perform the surgery. Get it?"

Max looked vaguely uncomfortable and his mouth

firmed. "Was your cowboy glad to have you back safe and sound last night?"

"He seemed happy enough to see me."

"I'll bet. What would he have done if I'd been a little late getting you home?" There was a surprisingly belligerent tone to Max's query.

"Beaten you to a pulp, probably. Now aren't you grateful I didn't stop off to have that drink at your hotel?" Sophy asked sweetly.

"I would have been willing to take my chances," Max told her softly.

Sophy blinked, startled by the quiet conviction in his voice. For a split second their eyes met in complete understanding. In Max's smoky gaze Sophy saw the answer to the question she had asked herself the night before. Max Travers would most definitely have made a pass at her if she'd gone to his hotel with him. That question answered, she was faced with the remaining one. What would she have done in response?

In that moment of frighteningly honest communication, Sophy had a terrifying premonition about the answer to that question, too. And she didn't like the way her nerves seemed to thrill to it. What on earth was wrong with her? It was impossible for her to be interested in Maximilian Travers. Desperately she tried to regain her composure, breaking off the intense eye contact.

"You might have been willing to take your chances, but I certainly wouldn't have been so willing," she said staunchly. "My parents would be furious if I sent you back to North Carolina in a pulped condition. They're already convinced I don't have enough respect for higher math as it is!"

"Maybe I could teach you a little respect for it," Max suggested whimsically. "Will you have dinner with me tonight?"

"Max, please . . ." Sophy felt suddenly very nervous, and it made her angry.

"The cowboy?"

"Nick is out of town. And I'd appreciate it if you'd stop calling him the cowboy!"

"You call me the wizard."

"So I do," she sighed. "Your logic is impeccable. Only to be expected from a professor of mathematics." Sophy waved the papers in her hand. "I'll see that these are ready by noon."

"Wednesday night?"

Sophy bit her lip. "Is that hotel room really so bad, Max?" Good heavens! Now what was she doing? Was she actually making excuses to see him again? Trying to convince herself that she felt sorry for him?

"Yes. The hotel room really is that bad."

"I'm busy Wednesday night," she heard herself say hesitantly. "But I might be able to make it for lunch sometime this week. Or . . . or a drink after work, perhaps." She must be feeling sorry for him. That was the only reason she could think of for agreeing to go out with him again now that her duty was done. But even as she made the uncertain suggestion, Sophy knew she was kidding herself.

"Thank you, Sophy, I'll look forward to lunch and a drink. Thursday for the lunch?" he asked calmly.

"Yes, well, I suppose . . ."

"Friday after work for the drink?"

"Max, I'm . . ." She broke off in annoyance. "Nick will be in town by then and we'll probably have plans for Friday evening."

"We'll discuss it Thursday at lunch," Max compromised smoothly. Then he turned around and walked out of the office without another word.

Sophy watched him go with a sense of foreboding. Then she slowly made her way back to her desk.

"You're going to type up Dr. Travers's notes, Sophy?" Marcie Fremont glanced at her co-worker. The dress was back in its box, safely stowed under Marcie's desk.

"Yes," Sophy mumbled, sitting down and arranging the work.

"Maybe you can learn something from them," Marcie observed. Marcie, in her efforts to climb the corporate ladder, was the kind of secretary who didn't just type up data, she studied what she typed. As a result she had an excellent working knowledge of the technical side of the company's business. So far, though, that knowledge hadn't done her much good in securing advancement.

"I doubt it," Sophy said. "It's very complicated. A lot of higher math. I'll be lucky to translate it. By the way, have you heard anything from Personnel yet?"

Marcie's mouth curved wryly. "Not a word. They're sure taking their time selecting someone for that position in Quality Control. I get the feeling they think it's a man's job."

"When the truth is, you could do it better than anyone else who's applied!"

"Thanks." Marcie smiled. "I needed that. What's with you and Dr. Travers, though? Did I hear you agreeing to have lunch with him?"

"He's a friend of my parents'. They all live back in North Carolina." Sophy busied herself with Max's notes.

"But he seems personally interested in you," Marcie persisted.

"He's just lonely. He's spending a few weeks here in Dallas, and I guess the hotel walls are closing in on him." And that was all it amounted to, she assured herself silently. That was all it could amount to. So why was she so damned aware of the man? Why was she anticipating, and yet nervous about, having lunch with him?

During the next two days Max seemed to be nearby every time Sophy turned around. He dropped by to check on the progress of his notes. He made a point of being in the building lobby when Sophy was leaving work. He somehow managed to go through the cafeteria line behind her when she was on morning break.

And when he wasn't around, Sophy realized she was unconsciously watching for him. A hundred times she lectured herself about the dangers of letting Dr. Max Travers get too close, and a hundred times she assured herself that she was only treating him like a family friend.

Late Wednesday afternoon, however, Sophy had cause to wish she had heeded her own lecture. She glanced up at a quarter to five as Max came toward her desk with a stack of papers and an intense, preoccupied air.

"Sophy, I hate to ask this, but I've got to have these done by eight tomorrow morning." He wasn't looking at her, rather at the notes in his hand, so he missed Sophy's horrified expression.

"Max! It's almost five o'clock! I can't possibly get those typed up today!"

"It's okay," he assured her absently as he arranged the papers on her desk. "I'm allowed to authorize overtime for you."

Sophy felt a wave of panic. "Max, I don't want any overtime. Not tonight. I've got a date with Nick. You know that. Maybe someone else . . ."

Max met her eyes very steadily across the width of the desk, and Sophy was startled by the cool, calculating expression in the depths of his smoky gaze. "Sophy, you know none of the other secretaries can handle this tonight. You're the only one with the vocabulary and the scientific background to get through this in an evening. Besides, you're the one who's been working on this project all along. It will take any of the others a couple of days to get up to speed, and I haven't got that much time." He tapped the folder on her desk with a pen he had removed from the pack in his shirt pocket.

"Max, I'm going out tonight. I just don't have the time. Maybe I could come in early tomorrow," she tried desperately. She was feeling trapped. For some reason it seemed absolutely imperative that she see Nick tonight. She needed to reassure herself about her relationship with him.

Sophy realized in a blinding flash of perception that she badly needed Nick Savage tonight as an antidote to Dr. Maximilian Travers.

Max shook his head at her suggestion. "I need the report typed up first thing in the morning for a meeting with S & J management. Don't make me pull rank, Sophy."

Rage swept through her. Sophy's chin came up and her eyes flashed with warning. "Rank, Dr. Travers? Exactly what kind of threat are you making?" Damn him!

Max leaned forward with an aggressiveness Sophy had not yet seen in him. His palms were spread flat on the desk, and it struck her that he had rather large, strong hands for an academician. Dangerous hands.

"Miss Bennet, may I remind you of what it's costing your company per day to engage my services? Your boss would not be pleased to have to pay for even one unnecessary day. When he discovered that that delay had ·been caused by the intransigence of one of his secretaries, I think he would be downright furious, don't you?"

Sophy went very still, watching him with bitter eyes. Max was absolutely right about her boss's reaction.

Frank Williams would be thoroughly angered if he thought her stubbornness had cost an extra day of Max's expensive time. He'd catch hell from his boss, and she'd probably wind up being the scapegoat.

And right at the moment, Sophy knew, she couldn't afford to lose her job. Too many of her future plans depended on the income.

But there was more involved here than her personal plans for the dress boutique and her association with Nick. Max was making it abundantly clear that on this level, at least, she was more or less in his power. And that thought alarmed her more than any other aspect of the situation. Instinctively she knew she should be putting as much distance between herself and Max as possible, not allowing herself to slip into such untenable situations as this one. But for the life of her, she couldn't see a way out. She took refuge in sarcasm.

"Ah, Dr. Travers, how quickly the facade of the gentle professor disappears. Give me your precious report. You'll have it by eight tomorrow."

Max's mouth twisted. "Sophy . . ."

"If that's an apology hovering on your lips, let's just forget about it, shall we, Dr. Travers? I'm not really all that surprised at the use of the threat, you know. I've known all my life that, in the pursuit of their goals, wizards have a way of not letting anyone or anything stand in their path. They have some notion that they are the elite and the rest of us should be only too happy to serve. My parents could be absolute tyrants when the occasion demanded."

"Sophy," Max tried again, "I'm sorry the occasion demanded I play the tyrant."

"I understand, Dr. Travers. And I'm sure you'll understand when I say that something has arisen which will make it impossible for me to have lunch with you tomorrow." It was a poor retaliation, but it was all she could manage on such short notice.

"What has arisen?" he shot back, eyes narrowing.

"Your academic arrogance. Excuse me, I'd better get started on these notes right away."

Damn it to hell, Sophy seethed as she began to work. Now she had to call Nick. He wasn't going to appreciate this. And she didn't want him mad at her. Not now. It was so important that he provide her with some reassuring evidence that she couldn't possibly have begun to fall for anyone as arrogant and as out of her world as Dr. Max Travers.

3

‿◦◦◦◦◦◦◦◦◦◦◦‿

He *had* been arrogant, Max admitted to himself an hour later as he carried a paper sack full of hamburgers and french fries and coffee up in the elevator to Sophy's floor.

Incredibly arrogant.

Sophy herself didn't even appreciate the full extent of his arrogance! He had deliberately set out to sabotage her date with the cowboy, and if she ever learned the truth there would be hell to pay. Much better to have her thinking he was simply pulling rank in order to get his project done.

For all the good it had done him.

Look at the price he was paying, Max chided himself. She'd canceled their lunch date tomorrow! But the convenient necessity of needing those notes typed up into a full-fledged report had seemed too good an opportunity to pass up.

Would she condescend to share the hamburgers with him? Since he was out lunch tomorrow, and since she had flatly refused to consider a break for dinner tonight, Max hadn't been able to think of any way to get a meal with her other than to bring in the fast food.

This evening was his one chance with Sophy, and he couldn't afford not to take advantage of it. He hoped the damned cowboy was frustrated as hell.

As he opened the door into the office, which was empty except for Sophy, Max braced himself for more of the ice treatment. He took a deep breath as she swung coldly accusing eyes on him for a fraction of a second and then returned to her work. She had been working with single-minded determination since she'd surrendered to his threat. Max's mouth hardened at the memory of how he had forced her to spend the evening with him. Then, for a moment, he simply drank in the sight of her, letting the pleasure of seeing her push out the uncertainties and feelings of guilt. What was it about Sophy that had attracted him from the first?

As usual, she made a vibrant splash of color against the subdued, neutral shades of the office decor. The curling mass of her hair was pulled back above her ears with wide yellow combs. Her outfit was a racy little yellow coatdress with lapels and cuffs in royal blue. Her narrow waist was cinched with a wide belt of blue leather trimmed with silver. As vivid as she was, Max was all too well aware that the attraction she held for him went far deeper than her appearance.

He was trained to see beneath the surface of things, but always before he had used that training in the realm of mathematics. With Sophy he wanted to use those skills in a new way. He wanted to know her completely. He wanted to secure her inner warmth and captivating *aliveness* for himself. Seeing her safely stuck behind the desk instead of dashing off to meet her cowboy gave him a feeling of untold satisfaction. Let tomorrow take care of itself. Tonight he had hours ahead with Sophy.

"I brought some hamburgers," he said on a determined note. She had to eat something, didn't she? "Since you insist on working through dinner, I feel obliged to make sure you get fed."

"Your consideration leaves me positively breathless, Dr. Travers." But she paused long enough to glance inside the sack. Then, to Max's relief, she withdrew a packet of french fries and began munching. Cautiously he sat down on the other side of her desk and reached for a burger.

"You can proofread the first section in a minute," she remarked shortly.

There was a long silence. "Was your cowboy very angry?" It was stupid to bring Nick Savage into the discussion, but Max suddenly had to know what the other man's reaction had been to the broken date.

"He wasn't thrilled."

Good, thought Max. Aloud he said, "I imagine he understands about the demands of your work."

There was another painful silence. When she failed to respond to the remark, Max decided to take the offensive. "Sophy, about our lunch date tomorrow . . ."

Her swivel chair swung around and she fixed him with a frozen glare. "Max, if you want this report done on time, you'll have to shut up and let me work. That was the whole point of the enforced overtime, wasn't it? To get this damn report out?"

He stifled a sigh and glanced down at what she had accomplished so far. "It looks like you're making good progress."

"I am." She swung the chair back around and returned to work.

"Well, in that case, we'll be able to knock off early and have a drink."

"My intention is to finish early and try to get to the party you forced me to miss this evening!"

Max froze. Damn it to hell! "Is your cowboy expecting you?"

49

"I'm going to surprise him. He said he was going to go anyway."

"I see. Sophy—"

"Shut up, Max, or you can damn well type this up yourself!"

"I don't know how to type," he retorted.

"Figures. I always thought they overlooked a few useful items in the education of wizards. I didn't get anything as useful as typing until I went off to college! Probably never let you waste much time playing with crayons, either, did they?"

"Well, no," Max replied bemusedly, "they didn't. I wasn't much interested in crayons, to tell you the truth. Why do you ask?"

"Never mind. Let me work."

Max hesitated a few minutes longer and then made his decision. It was time he met Nick Savage. "When you're done I'll drive you to the party," he stated gruffly. In that moment he couldn't have said exactly what made him want to see Sophy's lover. Max only knew that he had to find out what the other man was like. What did it take to attract Sophia Athena Bennet?

"That's not necessary, thank you," she said briskly.

"I don't want you taking the bus so late at night."

She glanced up in momentary surprise. "How did you know I took the bus this morning?"

"I, uh, just happened to see you come into work," he muttered, not meeting her eyes. Not for the world would he admit that when she came to work he was always standing at his office window, like a kid with his nose pressed to the candy store window.

"Well, don't worry. I've ridden the bus before at night," she assured him coolly.

"Sophy, I said I'll drive you to the party and that's final!" Was that him losing his temper? Good God!

She narrowed her eyes as if assessing his temper.

"Oh, all right, if it will make you happy. Anything to keep the expensive consultant in a good mood."

Max found himself torn between wanting to beat her and wanting to drag her down onto the floor and cover her body with his own. It was a bewildering and unfair tangle of emotions, and it clouded his normally very logical mind in an unfamiliar fashion.

By ten o'clock he could think of no further excuse to delay the inevitable. The report had been completed and proofed. It was perfect, and he knew Sophy was well aware of that fact. Time to meet the cowboy.

"I'll just freshen up in the ladies' room and then I'll be ready to go," Sophy said as she started for the door.

Max nodded bleakly behind her, watching as she disappeared down the hall. He did not want to turn her over to Nick Savage tonight, he realized. He wanted to take Sophy Bennet back to his hotel room and keep her there with him.

Max's mood became increasingly grim as he followed Sophy's chatty directions to one of the exclusive homes in the northern area of Dallas. Her mood was lightening in an inverse ratio to his own heavy frame of mind, he realized in disgust. She was looking forward to being with her cowboy.

"I'd like to come in with you and meet this guy," Max announced as he parked the Ford at the end of a long line of Lincolns, Cadillacs and Mercedeses.

"I don't see why you should want to meet Nick," Sophy began as she stepped out of the car.

"Curiosity," he told her flatly. "Put it down to sheer curiosity. Besides, if I like him I can always mention that to your parents. It might help them adjust to the shock of having a cowboy for a son-in-law." There was no way on earth he was going to like Nick Savage, of course, but Max saw no reason to mention that fact to Sophy, who was already watching him a bit warily.

"Well, I suppose there's no harm, but Max, there must be nearly two hundred people at this party tonight. It's going to take a while to find him in the crowd."

"I'll help you look," Max said smoothly, resisting the urge to say that the search might be difficult for him due to the fact that all cowboys looked alike.

"Oh, all right, if you insist," she muttered, too eager to find Nick to waste time arguing.

The party had clearly progressed beyond dinner to the steady drinking stage. Max and Sophy were virtually ignored as they came through the door. Max glanced around uneasily. Stetson hats, flared trousers and leather boots were everywhere. The crowd was lively, raucous and well on its way to a hangover.

"He said he was going to be here," Sophy muttered above the din. "The Everets are good friends of his."

Max watched her expressive profile as she searched the room. It would be nice to have Sophy search that earnestly for him, he thought grimly. That fantasy led to other, more fundamental fantasies, and he found himself disliking all cowboys intensely.

"A lot of people seem to have drifted out onto the back patio," Sophy said abruptly. "Let's try there."

With a sense of mounting irritation, Max followed as she cut a bright swath through the crowd. By the time he caught up with her again she had reached the flagstoned area at the rear of the house. The soft glow of lights from artfully styled lanterns illuminated a scene that seemed as crowded as the living room had been. Sophy singled out an elderly-looking man and got his polite attention at once.

"Nick Savage?" Max heard him say. "Thought I saw him a while ago with . . ." The elderly cowboy frowned and broke off hurriedly. "Uh, he was heading toward the pool, little lady. Yes, I do believe he was heading toward the pool." The man glanced up and sent Max a straight look. "You with this little lady here?"

"Yes I am," Max said firmly, ignoring Sophy's irritation.

"Well, then, I reckon that's okay, isn't it?" the other man said, clearly relaxing. "Yup, I think you might find Nick out by the pool." He winked at Max. "Might be a good idea to let him have a bit more time to himself, if you catch my drift."

Max heard the hint of warning in the stranger's voice, but Sophy appeared oblivious. She was already dragging him off toward the shadowy area around the huge, curving pool.

"Sophy . . ." Max started, and then stopped abruptly. A part of him instinctively wanted to urge caution, but another, more aggressive side wanted Sophy to push ahead and discover the possibly appalling truth. If he had understood what the older man had been trying to say, Max had a strong suspicion as to what Nick Savage was doing out by the pool. With a little luck the damn cowboy might obligingly condemn himself in Sophy's eyes.

"I don't see anyone," she complained as she hurried around the edge of the pool toward a row of shadowed cabanas. Then she stopped so suddenly Max nearly collided with her. An instant later he heard the soft sound. It was the unmistakable voice of a woman followed by the husky laughter of a man, and it emanated from the nearest cabana.

Before either of them could respond, the door of the cabana opened and Max looked up to see a man emerge, the same man who had emerged from the Lincoln the night he had taken Sophy home. Nick Savage had a pleased grin on his face, and he was just fastening his pants. In the moonlight the huge silver buckle of his belt gleamed obscenely.

"Nick." Sophy looked absolutely stricken. She stood

staring at the man, who appeared nearly as startled. As they faced each other, a woman emerged from the cabana. She was blond and beautiful and still getting dressed.

The four people involved in the dramatic tableau simply stared at each other for an endless moment. Max knew a shattering, wholly elemental satisfaction as the full ramifications of the scene came home to him. Nick Savage had been making love to the blond.

But even as he realized just how thoroughly the cowboy had compromised himself, Max was aware of a fierce desire to protect Sophy. He caught her wrist and pulled her back toward him. "Let's get out of here, Sophy," he growled.

"No!"

He heard the feminine shock and fury that underlined the single word.

"You bastard, Nick! You lying, cheating *bastard!* How could you do this to me? How dare you?"

Nick finally moved, disengaging himself from the blond, who had caught hold of his arm with a possessive grip. "Sophy, wait!"

"Friends of yours, Nicky dear?" the blond inquired with commendable aplomb as she adjusted her blouse. She ran a hand through her long hair. "I thought this was a private party. Just you and me." Deliberately she smiled.

Nick swore furiously, striding forward as if he would catch hold of Sophy. Max moved, yanking Sophy out of reach. She turned to him with a pleading, desperate look on her face.

"Max, please," she whispered raggedly. "Please take me home."

He didn't hesitate. "This way, Sophy." With sudden decision he tugged her around the pool, leaving the cowboy and his friend behind. Sophy followed mutely, seemingly grateful to have him take charge. She was still in shock, Max thought worriedly. Gently he helped her into the front seat of the Ford and then he slid in beside her, switching on the ignition. Was she all right? She looked so pale and frozen in the moonlight.

He guided the car down the winding drive to the road and started back toward downtown Dallas. If Sophy noticed she wasn't being driven home, she didn't seem to care. Max glanced at her stark, set profile. Was she furious or overwhelmed with grief? He hoped to God it was fury she was feeling.

"Sophy, I'm sorry you had to go through that scene back there."

"I thought he loved me, Max." She sounded so stricken; so listless. Max decided he could cheerfully strangle the cowboy. And then he thought about how Nick Savage had just ruined himself in Sophy's eyes.

"Maybe he does love you, Sophy. In his own way. Some men aren't very good at being faithful." What a bunch of bull that was, he told himself wryly. But he felt obliged to say something.

Her small hand doubled into a fist in her lap. "I could kill him."

"That makes two of us," Max muttered half under his breath.

"I trusted him, Max. I believed him when he said there was no one else. He's been making a complete fool out of me. What a stupid little idiot I've been."

Max didn't know what to say to that. In a way, he decided, she was absolutely right. Damned cowboy. "You need a drink," he stated.

"Several of them, I think. Oh, God, Max, this has got to be one of the most humiliating moments of my entire life!"

She said nothing more as he completed the drive to the hotel. He saw her blank, uncaring glance take in the fact that he was taking her to a lounge and not to her own home, and then she seemed to lose interest completely in her surroundings. Max was torn. On the one hand, he wanted to comfort her, but on the other he found himself aching to seize the opportunity. *The cowboy was no longer in the way.*

The cowboy was no longer in the way, he repeated to himself as he gently guided Sophy into the darkened lounge and seated her in a private corner. There he ordered drinks and watched as Sophy took great gulps of her Manhattan.

Never again, he told himself, would he be given the chance of getting this close to Sophia Athena Bennet. When she recovered her normal poise, she would once again put leagues of distance between them. But tonight she seemed to need him. Max sipped his drink patiently and waited.

"I don't understand it," Sophy finally mumbled sadly. "How could he do that to me? I thought we were building something. Something important. Oh, Max, I thought he was falling in love with me. I thought he wanted me."

Careful, Max told himself, don't come on too strong, or she'll turn the anger on you. Just be supportive. "I don't know why he would do it, Sophy. He doesn't deserve you, that's obvious. Probably thought he could have his cake and eat it, too."

She took another swallow of the Manhattan and stared at him over the rim, blue-green eyes huge and vulnerable. Max wanted to pull her into his arms to comfort her but didn't quite dare. Not yet.

"I could kill him," she repeated a bit violently.

"The thing to do," Max found the daring to advise, "is not waste another thought on him. There are other men, Sophy. Men who will appreciate you."

"All men are probably alike," she sniffed wretchedly.

"Sophy, you're smart enough to know that's not true."

56

"I don't feel smart at all at the moment. I feel as dumb as I used to feel back in school!"

"Feeling sorry for yourself?" he chided carefully.

"Yes, dammit!"

"Okay, okay," he soothed at once. "You're entitled, God knows. I just hate to see you wasting any more emotion on that creep. You're too good for him. You deserve someone who appreciates you!"

"Such as?" she challenged morosely.

Max sucked in his breath, watching her intently. "Such as me, Sophy."

"You!" She drew back, eyes widening. For a moment Max could have sworn he saw genuine, feminine panic in that bottomless gaze. Panic? Over him?

"I think you're the most fascinating woman I've ever met, Sophy." And that was no less than the truth, he realized.

She eyed him across the table, her expressive face revealing an indefinable emotion. What the hell was she thinking? He shouldn't have pushed so fast, Max admonished himself.

"It's very kind of you to try to make me feel better," she finally said in a small voice.

"Sophy, I'm not . . ."

"Could I have another drink, please?" she inquired with what sounded suspiciously like a sniffle.

He ordered, and they sat in silence while she sipped the second Manhattan a little more slowly than the first.

"It's sweet of you to be concerned, Max," she said at last in a polite little voice, "but I'll be all right, really I will. I feel like a fool at the moment, but I'm quite capable of looking after myself."

"Are you?"

"Oh, yes. We average types are really much better at handling the day-to-day shocks of life than you sheltered, ivory-tower geniuses. It's because you spend all your time wrapped up in your intellectual pursuits.

57

People like you never learn about the emotional side of life." She paused. "Maybe you're lucky."

"Because the emotional side of life can be painful?" he queried softly.

Her eyes glistened with unshed tears, and Max wanted to put his arms around her and let her cry out the pain she was clearly feeling.

"Yes," she whispered tightly. "Very painful. Oh, Max . . ."

He got to his feet at once and pulled her gently up beside him, holding her close with one arm while he signed the tab. "It's okay, Sophy," he murmured as he led her through the lobby. "It's okay, honey. Go ahead and cry. Get it out of your system. Then maybe you can start to forget him."

He kept up the soft monologue all during the ride in the elevator and the walk down the hall to his room. She clung to him and he took a strange, unfamiliar satisfaction in that. Sophy said nothing until he was turning the key in the door. Then she sniffed and moved restlessly within the curve of his arm.

"I should be getting home," she whispered a little dazedly, dashing the back of her hand across her eyes. "It's very nice of you to spend so much time with me, but . . ." The words trailed off on a small sob. "Maybe if I could wash my face?" She glanced up at him pleadingly.

"Right through there," Max said, inclining his head toward the bathroom door. God help him, his fingers were trembling. This was the first time he'd ever held her close, he thought. He watched her walk slowly across the room toward the bath. His hands were actually shaking!

She was here, right here in his hotel room. Now what?

Was she aware of where she was? Did she care? She

couldn't be drunk, not after only two drinks. But she was, perhaps, a bit drunk on her own humiliation and anger, he told himself.

It wouldn't be fair to take advantage of her under the present circumstances.

Not fair at all. Not the act of a gentleman and a scholar.

She was feeling lost and hurt and miserable and she was very, very vulnerable, Max told himself grimly. Damn it to hell, what was he thinking of doing? Taking advantage of Sophia Athena? Daughter of Paul and Anna Bennet? God forbid.

He'd probably get no further than trying to kiss her, he told himself angrily as he stalked across the room to find the bottle of complimentary champagne that the hotel had sent up when he'd arrived. It was where he had stuck it, safely stored in the small refrigerator. Moodily he removed it and began to open it.

She'd probably turn all her fury and pain on him if he even so much as tried to take her in his arms and kiss her. He poured the champagne.

But she was so weak and vulnerable right now. She might not realize his intentions until it was far too late. The champagne tasted strange. He glared down at the bubbling stuff in the glass in his hand. Simultaneously he heard the sound of running water from the bath. How long would she be in there? Max wondered. He tried another sip of the drink and stared at his reflection in the mirror.

He didn't look anything like a cowboy, and Sophia preferred cowboys. Or she had until tonight, he reminded himself savagely. Then Max groaned. He wasn't likely ever to get another chance with Sophy Bennet and he knew it. Never again would he have her all to himself in a hotel room. Never again was he likely to find himself cast in the role of comforter.

What if he abused the unique position in which he found himself tonight? What if he actually managed to get her into bed? His palms went abruptly damp.

"She'd hate my guts in the morning," he told his reflection with grim certainty. *God help him, he wanted her.*

Max winced and turned away from the too-revealing mirror. She'd hate him even more than she hated that cowboy.

But he'd never get another chance like this. Max was so certain of that. If he didn't take advantage of the situation, he'd never know what it was like to make love to the most intriguing woman he'd ever met. He'd never wanted a woman so badly in his life. What in hell was the matter with him?

His fingers tightened around the stem of the champagne glass. How could he make himself walk away now from the glittering temptation that had been put in his path? God help him, he was only a man, regardless of how often she called him a wizard.

Was having Sophy tonight worth the risks of incurring her fury in the morning?

Damn it, the answer was yes. He downed the last of the champagne, staring out the window with unseeing eyes. What if he could make it so good for her that she wouldn't remember their time together with rage? What if he managed to show her just how much he needed her? There was a streak of compassion in her, a gentleness that might temper her anger. If she realized how much he needed her, perhaps she would be kind to him in the morning. Perhaps she would stay with him. . . .

The door to the bathroom opened on that dangerously tantalizing thought. He turned abruptly to find Sophy framed in the doorway. She looked so miserable and bleak. And it was all that stupid cowboy's fault.

"I could kill him."

"What?" She glanced at him in confusion, and Max realized he'd spoken aloud. He shook his head and walked stiffly across the room to put a glass of champagne in her hand.

"I said I could kill him. Except that he's not worth the trouble. Sophy, you're better off without him. You'll realize that eventually."

"I suppose you're right." Wistfully she took the champagne and sat down on the edge of the bed, smiling wanly. "It's just so hard to admit how stupid I've been. I *trusted* him, Max."

"You weren't stupid." He sat down carefully beside her and put his arm around her. She accepted the proffered comfort, leaning her head against his shoulder. "You thought you were in love and you thought he loved you."

"It could have been worse," Sophy mumbled, sipping the champagne.

"Worse?"

"I think I would have felt even worse if . . . if Nick and I had been lovers," she mumbled into the glass.

Max stifled a surge of satisfaction, barely managing to keep his tone neutral. "You mean you weren't sleeping with him?"

She shook her head. "Maybe that's why he turned to that blond," she chastised herself. "Maybe I shouldn't have kept him waiting."

"Sophy, you mustn't blame yourself."

"But I . . ."

Max cut off the self-castigating flow of words with his fingers on her lips. "No. Sophy, he's the one who cheated on you. None of this is your fault. You're the wronged party in this mess. Remember that."

Her wide blue-green eyes stared at him as he continued to press her mouth gently with his hand. Was that a flicker of awareness he saw in her gaze? Was it possible she might want him just a little?

61

"Oh, God, Sophy . . ."

On a low groan of barely controlled need, he removed the glass from her hand.

"Max? Max, I'm not sure . . ."

"Hush, Sophy. Don't think about anything. Just relax and let me comfort you. Please, honey. It's all I want to do." It was the truth and it was a lie and Max didn't know how to explain it.

Slowly, half-afraid she might disappear in his grasp if he moved too quickly, Max lowered his mouth to feather her parted lips with his own. She didn't move as he made exquisitely exciting contact. He felt the tiny tremor that went through her, however, and somehow it fueled his own carefully contained desire. At least she wasn't totally indifferent to him, he thought exultantly.

"Relax, Sophy, just relax. Let me hold you until you forget him." He didn't know where the soothing words were coming from. They seemed half-instinctive, the calming, gentling words men had used from the beginning of time to tame nervous women.

She tensed as he drew her slowly backward onto the quilted bedspread. He sensed she was about to resist and he didn't know what else to do except chain her with another kiss. His mouth closed more deliberately over hers and he heard a faint moan from far back in her throat. The sound made the urgent longing in him all the more insistent. A part of her did want him, damn it!

"Max, no, I don't . . ." Her head shifted restlessly on the quilt as she freed her mouth.

"I always seem to find myself looking for ways to shut you up," he muttered hoarsely, yanking off his glasses and tossing them heedlessly onto the nightstand. For a second he stared down at her, glorying in the knowledge that there was a tiny, faltering flame in her now. She trembled again as she met his gaze, and with a rasping exclamation Max lowered his head to plunge his tongue deeply into her mouth.

Instinctively he used his weight to pin her more securely to the quilt. Her slender body was still stiff and uncertain beneath him, but he could feel the thrusting softness of her breasts. She felt so good lying there under him. He pushed his lower body strongly against her thighs, seeking to let her know the extent of his own arousal.

"Max!" It was a soft cry, torn from her when he freed her mouth temporarily to explore the sensitive place behind her ear.

"Hush, Sophy. Just relax and trust me tonight. I'll take care of you. I'll make you forget him. By morning you'll only think of me, I swear it."

4

Sophy's senses seemed to be spinning. Not in a mad, frightening whirl, but in a deliciously intriguing manner. Everything was suddenly right. The moment Max had taken her in his arms, everything had become right.

The restless uncertainty, the attraction she had been experiencing, the indefinable aura about Max that made her so totally aware of him were suddenly explained. Fully explained.

She wanted him.

The realization was too startling to deal with on an intellectual level tonight. Sophy wanted only to give herself up to the sweeping feelings of the moment. Her emotions felt raw, and Max's arms promised soothing safety. There would be time enough in the morning to consider what she was doing.

With a sigh of longing that had been suppressed since she had first set eyes on Max Travers, Sophy pushed aside all thoughts of the future and surrendered to the wonder of the moment.

This was what had been missing all along in her relationship with Nick Savage: this marvelous *rightness,* this sensation of need and the promise of shared satisfaction. This soft, sweet longing was a totally new and unexplored element in her life, and it was all bound up with Max Travers. In that moment Sophy was absolutely certain the emotions she was experiencing could not exist without Max as their focus.

It made no sense and yet it made all the sense in the world.

Sophy sighed against Max's mouth, a sensation of thrilling languor flowing through her. Her leg moved slightly on the bedspread, and Max's thigh covered it, pressing down firmly, trapping it.

"I want to be your lover tonight, Sophy. I want to hold you and make you forget that damned cowboy," Max growled against the skin of her throat.

"I don't want to think about him," she agreed fervently, sinking her fingertips into the dark brown depths of his hair. "You're the only one I seem to be able to think about at the moment." She heard him draw in his breath quite sharply and knew a distinct sense of satisfaction. He wanted her. Max wanted her as much as she wanted him.

"That cowboy is a fool!"

"Oh, Max . . ."

"Any man who would risk losing you just for the sake of a quickie at a party has got to be a fool."

"Please, Max. I don't want to talk about him."

Max cradled her in one arm as he stretched out slowly beside her on the bed. His other hand began to move with sureness and wonder on her body. The soothing words he murmured contained a tense urgency, a sense of demand that was at once wholly masculine and completely enthralling.

"Let me touch you, darling. Sophy, honey, you feel so good under my hands. So very good."

Sophy shifted restlessly, closing her eyes as her body warmed under his touch. When Max buried his lips in her throat, letting her feel the edge of his teeth, she shivered.

"Sophy! Sophy, I want you. I need you tonight. I have to keep you here with me." He shaped her breast with exploring fingers and she whispered his name.

"Max . . . I feel so strange. I've never felt like this before. Oh, Max, what have you done to me?" Sophy asked wonderingly. Her arms went around him almost convulsively.

"Ah, sweetheart, you're so warm and soft and vibrant. You're all the colors of the rainbow. Did you know that? All the colors that have been missing in my life. I want to see you shimmer in my arms. I want to make you even more alive than you already are!" Max groaned again, his voice raw and husky. He found the buckle of the wide blue leather belt and undid it with deliberate movements.

Sophy could feel his body straining against hers as he slowly, carefully undressed her. The full, waiting male power of him was electrifying. As the yellow dress fell aside, he curved his hand around her buttocks and pulled her tightly against him. Sophy shuddered in helpless response.

"Feel how much I want you," he grated.

Her nails dug into the strongly contoured muscles of his back, and she found herself pressing closer, inhaling the satisfying scent of his body. The yellow dress seemed to have disappeared of its own accord, and a moment later the lacy little bra went the same route. All she wore now was a small triangle of satin.

"You're so incredibly exciting," Max growled in wonder as he bent his head to kiss her breast. "Just looking at you across a room is exciting. But having you here in my bed is almost unbelievable."

"Oh!" Sophy flinched in thrilling reaction as he drew

her sensitized nipple into his mouth. Tiny shivers of pleasure pulsated through her, and she began to murmur his name over and over again. The nipple hardened at once beneath the compelling touch of his rasping tongue.

"So responsive," he breathed. "You must want me, Sophy. Please say you want me."

"Yes, Max," she whispered obediently. "I want you."

His palm was gliding down the warm skin of her stomach, and she writhed under the touch with the uninhibited pleasure of a cat being stroked. The prowling, tantalizing fingers slid down her thigh and up along the silken inside to the point where the satin underpanties barred his path. Sophy's knee flexed convulsively, her toes curling tightly.

"You're safe here with me, sweetheart," he murmured as he slipped his finger under the elasticized edge of the panties and began to touch her in the most thrilling manner. The patterns he wove at the center of her softness made her cry out in wonder and delight.

"Please, Max. Please . . ."

The urge to touch him more intimately came upon her in a rush, and suddenly Sophy was pulling at the knot of his narrow tie, yanking at the buttons of his shirt and fumbling with the buckle of his belt.

"Yes, darling, yes," he muttered, shrugging out of the shirt. He caught her fluttering hands when she would have paused to explore the expanse of his hair-roughened chest. "Finish undressing me, honey."

Sophy did as he demanded and a moment later he lay beside her, totally nude. She gasped with pleasure and flexed her fingers like tiny claws against the bronzed skin of his sleek body.

"God, Sophy, I feel like I'm burning up."

"Oh, Max, you're so . . . so . . ." She couldn't take her eyes off his aroused, utterly masculine body.

"So what?" he taunted softly with a shaky laugh. "So

desperate for you? So full of aching desire that I hurt? I am, darling. Only you can give me any relief tonight. I've been wanting you since the first moment I saw you. I've never known such a hunger for a woman. You've got to satisfy me or I'll go out of my head. I can't wait any longer for you."

He sprawled suddenly across her with undeniable intent, forcing her thighs apart with his own. His hands closed over her shoulders, anchoring her firmly beneath him, and he lay looking down at her with a fire blazing in his eyes.

"Max, wait . . ." Too late Sophy realized it had all gone too far. Everything was spinning out of control. Her body was filled with sensual longing and her head was filled only with the desire to respond to Max's urgent demands.

"No, darling, I can't wait," he gritted with unexpected savagery as he covered her. "If I wait, I'll lose you." He blocked the words in her mouth with his lips and then he moved aggressively against her.

He was so heavy, Sophy thought. Heavy and hard and irresistible. God, how she wanted him. Her own body was shivering with reaction and desire.

"Put your arms around me and hold on to me," he ordered thickly. "I'll keep you safe, Sophy. Just hold on to me."

Blindly she obeyed, clinging to him as if he were her only source of security, even as a part of her dimly recognized that he was really the source of a threat unlike any she had ever known. Then he forged into her damp, heated softness, bringing a breathless cry of surrender into her throat. Greedily he swallowed the small sound. For a moment they both lay locked together in a kind of shock at the completeness of the union. Then slowly, powerfully, Max began to move.

Sophy was utterly lost. Never had she known such exquisite, almost terrifying passion. It captivated and compelled and controlled. She could no more have escaped it now than she could have stopped the earth in its orbit. Max held her, taking everything she had to give and rewarding her with the gift of himself. It was unbelievably primitive, an act of fire and passion, and it came to an end in a shivering culmination that had Sophy's nails leaving small wounds on Max's back. Her whole body tightened with the exploding release, and even as she gave herself up to it, Sophy heard Max's shout of heady satisfaction as he followed her over the edge.

For long, endless moments Sophy allowed herself to drift on the outgoing tide of passion. Vaguely aware of the warmth of Max's perspiration-damp body, she listened to the sound of his breathing as it settled back into a normal pattern. His thigh still sprawled across her legs, holding her immobile.

She didn't want to open her eyes, she realized. She wanted only to go on drifting forever in this pleasant, safe realm where reality could not reach her.

"Go to sleep, Sophy," Max drawled in her ear. "Just relax and go to sleep. We can talk it all out in the morning."

The command fit in very well with her own desire to avoid the reality of what had happened. Sophy closed her eyes and obeyed.

It was a faint sound in the hall outside the room that awakened her several hours later. For a moment Sophy lay perfectly still, trying to orient herself, and then she became violently aware of Max's hard thigh lying alongside her own soft one. Her head turned on the pillow to stare at his shadowed face. He was sound asleep.

The sound outside in the hallway registered. It was merely the scraping of a key in the lock of the room next door.

My God, Sophy thought, sitting up slowly. *What have I done?*

She stared down at herself as the sheet fell aside, and she knew a sense of shock at her own nakedness. How could she have been so weak? Nervously she looked down at Max's bare chest as he lay sprawled on his back.

He lay beside her like some ancient conquering hero. There was an arrogance in the lean, sleek lines of his body that she had never noticed before. But that was because she had always seen him in the camouflage of his academic uniform, Sophy thought on a note of hysteria. He had used the old-fashioned white shirt, the little nerd pack, the glasses and the corduroy trousers to get close to her the way a hunter stalks his prey in camouflaged clothing.

Maximilian Travers had promised comfort and given her passion instead.

Even with Nick Savage, Sophy thought grimly, she hadn't been so stupid.

But she had always lost out to wizards. All her life she had been unable to hold her own against them. This time was no different, except that a part of her had always felt that this was an area of life in which wizards would never be a threat.

Sophy's hands clenched in small fists as she continued to stare down at Max. She had to get out of there. Max was everything he had no right to be: strong, virile, dominant. And brilliant. She must get away from him as quickly as possible.

The damned wizard had deliberately taken advantage of her, Sophy told herself ruthlessly as she pushed aside the sheet and slid off the bed. Yes, that was what had happened. He had used her. Taken advantage of her emotional vulnerability last night. She was torn between a fierce desire to pound him with her hands and the equally strong desire to flee.

She elected flight.

With painful caution Sophy searched for her clothing, scrambling awkwardly into her underwear and the yellow coatdress. She found her shoes under the bed. In the end she couldn't find her belt, however, and she didn't want to waste any more time searching for it. She dressed hurriedly, her only goal to escape from the scene of her stupidity. No, damn it! Not stupidity. *Vulnerability.* It was her own vulnerability that had gotten her into this situation.

After running a hand through her heavy, tangled curls, Sophy checked for her small purse and then headed for the door. It was almost five o'clock according to the digital clock beside the bed. To her great relief, Max didn't stir as she let herself out into the hall. Cautiously, knowing she couldn't bear to face him at that moment, she shut the door behind her and hurried downstairs to find a cab.

Max watched her leave through slitted eyes. There was no point in calling out to her. She was running away from him.

"Hell," he muttered in the darkness as the door closed softly behind her. "Damn it to hell." She hadn't even waited until morning to leave him. She probably hated him.

With a groan, he sat up in bed and switched on the bedside lamp. Almost instantly his eyes fell on the familiar outline of her wide leather belt. Reaching down, he picked it up and then pushed his glasses onto his nose. For a long moment he simply sat staring at it. Cinderella had left her calling card, but he didn't need to be told that she didn't view him as a prince.

Such a slender little waist, he thought, fingering the belt. And such beautiful, flaring thighs below that tiny waist. Darn it, his body was hardening just at the memory!

Max stood up with a muttered groan. He had about

as much chance of getting Sophy Bennet back in his bed as he did of flying to the moon. Less. Then his hand tightened on the belt. Hadn't he been just as pessimistic about his chances with Sophy before that cowboy had been so obligingly dumb?

And she *had* responded to him last night, Max reminded himself resolutely as he headed toward the bathroom. Responded, hell. That was putting it mildly. She had been like molten gold in his arms. Would she try to deny it if he confronted her with that fact this morning? Probably. Reminding her of how she had surrendered in his arms would not be a gentlemanly thing to do. But he had to convince her that there was something between them, and he could think of no other way.

On the opposite side of town, Sophy dressed for work with equally grim intent. In her mind she planned wildly different strategies for dealing with Max Travers. No sense pretending she could avoid him. The company wasn't that large and he would probably seek her out, anyway. Would he gloat about her surrender?

A part of her wanted to rail at him like a wronged woman, but another part wanted to maintain some sense of dignity. After all, she was twenty-eight years old. Dignity was crucial. It was about all she had left.

Half an hour early, she made her way into the office wearing a pinstriped dress trimmed with white collar and cuffs. It was the most severely styled dress in her wardrobe, designed primarily for weddings and funerals. It gave her a sense of aloof arrogance, however, and she badly needed that this morning. There was no one else around, so she occupied herself with brewing coffee. She was watching it drip into the pot when the door opened and Max walked into the room.

For an instant Sophy just stared at him, terribly

unprepared for the confrontation. It was too soon. She needed more time, she thought nervously. Max was back in his familiar clothing but it didn't help. Sophy knew she would never forget the man underneath those unthreatening garments. All the camouflage in the world wouldn't serve to hide Max Travers from her eyes now.

"Good morning, Max. Come for a cup of coffee?" Sophy forced a breezy little smile from out of nowhere. Damn it, she would not let herself be intimidated. She had stopped being intimidated by wizards years ago, and Sophy told herself she had no intention of going back to those feelings of intimidation now.

He walked steadily across the room until he was standing beside her. His smoky eyes watched her intently behind the shield of his glasses. "I could use a cup, yes, thank you."

"Here you go," she said briskly, pouring out two cups and handing him one. "All set to discuss your preliminary report with management?"

He blinked warily. "What report?"

"Oh, you remember, Max," she said very sweetly. "The one you kept me working on until nearly ten last night."

A slow stain of red spread across his cheeks. "Uh, yes, I'm ready."

"Good. I wouldn't want to think the *entire* evening had been a waste. Heaven knows a good chunk of it certainly was. Nice to know something was salvaged." Darn it! She would not allow him to revel in her reactions to him last night. She would make him think it meant nothing. Absolutely nothing.

"Sophy . . ."

"Yes, Max?"

"Sophy, about last night," he began decisively.

"Max, you're supposed to be a very bright man. I

should think you'd have enough intelligence not to discuss last night." Her tone was one of mild amusement, and Sophy was proud of it. But her blue-green eyes were swirling with chilled fury.

Max's face hardened. "You know as well as I do that we can't ignore last night."

"Why not? It seems like an excellent idea to me!"

"Damn it, Sophy. Stop acting like a brittle little creature whose emotions don't run any deeper than icing on a cake!"

"How do you know that's not exactly how deep my emotions run?" she challenged tightly.

"Because you showed me how deep the passion runs in you last night. And if the passion is that deep, so are the rest of your emotions!" he suddenly blazed.

"Your degrees are in mathematics! Not amateur psychology!" she stormed. "All you saw in me last night was desire!"

"The hell I did," he ground out coldly. "You gave yourself completely last night, Sophy Bennet. You gave yourself to me. Surrendered to me. I know the difference between temporary desire and real passion."

"How could you? You're only a mathematician!"

His mouth crooked in a strange little smile that faded almost instantly. "You taught me the difference, Sophy. You have only yourself to blame."

"Don't you dare blame last night on me!" she cried. "You took advantage of me! I was feeling emotionally weak and vulnerable. I'd had a great shock. You were supposed to be a friend. You said you wanted to comfort me. I trusted you."

"Sophy, all of that may have been true up to a point . . ."

"Nice of you to take a little responsibility for what happened!"

"I take full responsibility for what happened," he

returned gently. "But that doesn't change the basic fact that you surrendered last night, sweetheart. You came to me with no reservations and you gave yourself completely. I've never had a woman give herself to me like that. And now that I've had you, you can't expect me to let you just walk away saying it was only a case of temporary attraction."

"That's all it was! And you had no right to take advantage of me! Hardly the action of a gentleman and a scholar!" she seethed, grasping at the only insult available.

"I know." He offered no excuses, no explanations. He just admitted it.

"Damn you!" Sophy lost her frail temper completely and flung the rapidly cooling contents of her coffee cup all over his white shirt and narrow nerd tie.

For an instant they stared at each other in ominous, shocked silence, and into that frozen setting walked Marcie Fremont. Her blue eyes widened briefly in surprise as she took in the highly charged scene.

"I'm sorry. Excuse me, please." Politely she turned to walk back out the door through which she had just entered, but Sophy reached it ahead of her, flinging it open and racing madly down the hall toward the ladies' room.

She was vaguely aware of Marcie staring after her in concerned astonishment and she thought she heard Max angrily calling her name, but Sophy didn't stop until she was safely behind the door of one of the few refuges allowed modern woman.

Instantly she began to regret her lack of self-control. Hastily she dabbed at her eyes with a damp paper towel. How could she have made such a fool of herself in front of Marcie? Marcie was always so perfectly controlled. The scene would undoubtedly be all over the office within an hour.

No, perhaps not. Marcie Fremont was not a gossip. She was too conscious of her professional image to lower herself to common office gossip. Thank heavens it had been Marcie who had walked in on that horrible confrontation with Max. If it had been Karen or Sandy or Steve or Peter, the rumor mill would already be humming.

The door to the rest room opened and Sóphy glanced up.

"Are you all right?" Marcie Fremont asked seriously.

"Yes. Yes, I'm fine."

"I'm awfully sorry about walking in on you and Dr. Travers like that."

"You could hardly have known what was going on." Sophy smiled shakily.

"Dr. Travers said you were a little upset about something that happened last night. Anything I can do? Does it involve you and your friend Nick Savage?"

"It's all tied up in one big mess, but no, there's nothing you can do, Marcie." Sophy sighed.

"Dr. Travers seemed very concerned."

"He should be! It's all his fault!"

"I see." Marcie hesitated a moment, watching as Sophy finished dabbing at her eyes. "Look, you don't have to worry about my saying anything, Sophy."

Sophy smiled her gratitude. "Thank you, Marcie. It's very kind of you to be so discreet."

"Dr. Travers asked me to have you call him when you've, uh, recovered," Marcie added gently.

"Dr. Travers can wait until the sixth dimension freezes over before I call him about anything," Sophy hissed, her temper flaring. "The bastard. I thought Nick was a bastard. He could take lessons from Dr. Maximilian Travers. God, Marcie, right now I don't care if I never date another man again!" Taking a deep breath, Sophy shook back her curling mane and fixed a grim little smile on her face. "I guess I'd better get back to work. Thanks," she mumbled again in helpless gratitude for the other woman's support and discretion.

"If you're sure you're all right?"

"I'm madder than hell, but I'm all right."

Marcie relaxed with a faint smile. "I guess today is going to be a traumatic day for both of us, one way or another."

Sophy arched an eyebrow inquiringly. "Personnel is going to make the decision?"

Marcie nodded, her excitement barely suppressed. "I heard they were going to announce the name of the person who's going to get that job in Quality Control. Oh, Sophy, I'm so nervous. . . ."

"Marcie, you know you're the most qualified person for that job. You've got your business administration degree, and you've been assisting Quality Control on all those special tasks since you arrived. You've got a real working knowledge of what they're doing down there in QC!"

"Well, we'll find out today if Personnel sees things that way!"

Both women walked back to the office with determined resolve. Max had had the sense to depart.

When he made the mistake of calling at ten o'clock, Sophy didn't even bother to return his cautious greeting.

"Sorry, wrong number," she said sweetly, and replaced the receiver. "Arrogant wizard," she muttered as she hung up.

Max called again at eleven and she repeated the action. When he tried again at twelve it was Marcie who answered the phone, and as soon as she made eye contact with Sophy, the blond said, "I'm sorry, Dr. Travers, she just stepped out for a few minutes. I'll tell her you called."

Max showed up in person, however, right after lunch, advancing on Sophy's desk with a determined expression and a file of notes in his hand.

"Some revisions to that report you did for me last night," he stated without giving her a chance to react verbally to his unwanted presence. "They came out of this morning's meeting."

"Nice of you not to bring them by at five and order me to stay late to finish them," Sophy observed coldly.

"I had a feeling you might not be interested in working overtime this evening," he admitted dryly.

"You're quite right. I worked far too much of it last night."

He frowned and leaned forward, apparently conscious of Marcie sitting nearby where she could overhear the conversation. "I'd like to talk to you. Privately."

"Go to hell, Dr. Travers," Sophy gritted with an artificial smile.

"I'll take you out to dinner tonight," he continued roughly.

"I'm afraid that's impossible. I have other plans."

"Don't give me that. I know damn well you don't have a date tonight."

"You're wrong, Dr. Travers," Sophy retorted as inspiration struck. "I'm having a drink with Marcie after work. Aren't I, Marcie? We're going to celebrate Marcie's new promotion." She turned in her swivel chair and looked at her co-worker, eyes pleading for support.

"If the promotion comes through, we'll be celebrating it," Marcie said quickly. "If not we'll be having a consolation drink."

Max glared at Sophy and then at Marcie. Both women met his look with bland smiles. He was beaten for the moment and he was wise enough to know it. He turned on his heel and stalked out of the office without another word. A long, charged silence hovered in his wake. Then Marcie spoke.

"I'd really be quite happy to have a drink with you, Sophy."

"Thank you. I have a hunch we'll both need it."

"Yes."

The news about the promotion arrived just before five o'clock. It came in the form of a brief call from Personnel to Marcie. Even as Sophy watched her friend's face become closed and withdrawn, she knew what the verdict was. Marcie thanked the caller with distant politeness and hung up the phone, her eyes glacier cold and filled with anger and disappointment.

"Oh, Marcie . . ." Sophy began sympathetically, knowing how much the job had meant to the other woman.

"They gave it to Steve Cameron," Marcie whispered. "Steve Cameron. He doesn't even have a business degree. He hasn't had the experience I've had working on QC projects. His only recommendation for that job is that he's a man."

"They're fools to give it to him. That man is all self-hype and no genuine ability!" Sophy said with sudden, fierce loyalty to Marcie. "God, if there's one thing I learned to recognize at a tender age, it's real ability. Believe me, Cameron doesn't have it. Idiots!"

"Oh, God, Sophy. I was counting on that job. When I took this position in the secretarial pool they more or less promised me that it would only be temporary. It was understood it was only to last until something better came up for which I was qualified! And I was qualified for that promotion, damn it!" Marcie's hand curled into a small fist.

Sophy bit her lip and then started shoving her unfinished work into drawers. "Come on, Marcie. Let's get out of here. Both of us have had enough for one day."

"It's not quite five," Marcie said automatically.

"Who the hell cares!"

The cocktail lounge they found nearby was just beginning to fill up with an after-work crowd. The hum of conversation provided a pleasant cover for Sophy and Marcie's grim discussion. Secluded at a small booth toward the back, they ordered margaritas and considered the circumstances in which they found themselves.

Under the influence of the bond cemented between them that day, Sophy found herself telling Marcie the whole sordid story of her night with Max. She explained the humiliating scene with Nick, the way Max had offered comfort and the way he had taken advantage of her emotional vulnerability.

Marcie listened compassionately, and then she poured out her own frustrations with trying to make it up the corporate ladder in what was still essentially a man's world.

"There are times when old-fashioned words like *revenge* sound very sweet," Sophy finally announced over the second margarita. "I've been having daydreams of revenge all day."

"I've been having them off and on for five years," Marcie admitted wryly. "Every time I got my fingers stepped on whenever I tried to climb the ladder. Darn it, I think this time I've had enough. . . ."

She let the words trail off and Sophy looked at her curiously. "What are you talking about, Marcie?"

The other woman hesitated, and Sophy had the feeling she was carefully assessing her next words. Then she gave Sophy a very level glance. "Would you honestly like a chance at punishing Dr. Maximilian Travers?"

"I'd give anything to be able to teach him a lesson for what he did to me last night," Sophy heard herself whisper savagely. "But I don't see how that's possible. What could I possibly do to Max to repay him for what he did to me last night?"

"You could join me in what I have planned for S & J Technology," Marcie said simply. Setting aside her drink, she leaned forward and told Sophy exactly what revenge could mean and how it could be taken.

5

The following evening Sophy stood in the corridor outside Max's hotel room, her hand lifted to knock. At the last moment she almost changed her mind. In an agony of suspense she let her knuckles hover just above the door panel.

It would be simple to turn around and forget the whole thing. But deep down she knew what she had to do. With a sigh, she rapped her hand gently against the door.

"Who is it?" Max called impatiently from within.

"Room service," she muttered, not feeling like yelling out her name. There was the sound of a phone being dropped into its cradle, and a few seconds later the door was swung inward.

"I didn't order any . . . Sophy!" Max stared at her, his eyes narrowing in wary surprise. His tie was hanging loose and his dark hair looked as though he'd been running his fingers through it. "What the hell are you doing here? I've been trying to call you all evening!"

"Would you rather I turned around and went home to wait for your call?" she murmured sullenly.

"Don't be ridiculous. Come in." Max reached out to grasp her by the shoulder, tugging her into the room and slamming the door shut behind her as if afraid she might escape. Then he released her and leaned back against the door. His eyes roved hungrily over the narrow white skirt and safari-style shirt she wore, and Sophy could guess the memories he was recalling. She edged away from him, moving across the room toward a chair. She refused to glance at the bed.

"You must be wondering why I'm here," she began, feeling a wave of unease as she realized she was back at the scene of her debacle. Max must have seen the expression on her face, because he levered himself away from the door and motioned to the chair near the window.

"Please sit down," he invited gruffly. "I'll order something from room service." He picked up the phone.

"Make mine tea," she drawled, sinking into the chair with what she hoped was nonchalance. "I had a little problem handling my liquor the last time I was here, so I'd just as soon not take any chances."

One of Max's dark brows lifted tauntingly. "Going to blame everything on the fact that you had too much to drink? You weren't really drunk and you know it, Sophy."

"Tea," she repeated, disdaining to argue with him.

Max's mouth hardened but he ordered a pot of tea for two. Then he came slowly toward her to take the chair on the other side of the small oval table. "You've been ignoring my calls all day. When I came to see you at lunch you claimed you were eating with your friend Marcie. When I asked you to have dinner with me last night you said you had plans with Marcie. When I tried to contact you this afternoon you had someone say

83

you'd been sent across town on an errand. All that avoidance and now you show up on my doorstep." He ran a hand through his hair. "Why, Sophy?"

"Why have you been trying so hard to see me?" she countered coolly.

"You know damn well why!"

"You're feeling guilty?"

"Guilt doesn't enter into it," he gritted. "I want you."

"You've had me," she reminded him gently.

"Stop trying to be so darn blasé about the whole thing."

"What exactly do you want from me, Max? Another toss in the hay? A few evenings in bed to help relieve the boredom while you're in Dallas?"

"Sophy, you're trying to twist everything."

"Shall I put a more sophisticated label on it? Do you want an *affair* with me, Max?"

"Yes, damn it, I do!" he exploded.

"Ah." She nodded. "Marcie was right." Sophy leaned back into her chair while Max eyed her warily.

"Marcie?" he finally asked cautiously.

"Ummm. She told me she thought you wanted a full-scale affair. Said she could tell by the way you watched me run out of the office the other morning when she walked in on us. Marcie, you'll be interested to know, is a very shrewd woman. Has her eye on the highest levels of corporate management. And she knows a lot about what motivates people. Probably going to be very successful someday."

"Stop playing with me, Sophy. Are you here because Marcie said I wanted to go on sleeping with you? Believe me, that analysis didn't take any great intelligence on her part. Any moron could tell I want you."

Sophy flushed in spite of her determination to remain serenely cool. "You weren't the only one Marcie Fremont analyzed. She had the astuteness to also realize that I was thirsting for revenge." Max looked startled at the matter-of-fact way Sophy announced the information. "But, then, she's a woman," Sophy continued coolly. "Probably only another woman could understand the wish for revenge in a situation such as this."

"Sophy . . ." Max began dangerously.

"Which brings us to my reason for being here tonight," she interrupted evenly.

"Revenge?" His smoky eyes were chilled.

"She suggested an interesting method, Max. Marcie proposed I continue with the affair. She thought I should show up on your doorstep tonight and admit that I simply couldn't stay away from your bed. She said I should imply I had been so overwhelmed by your virility and prowess in bed that I simply had no other choice but to surrender completely."

"Your friend Marcie seems to know her way around the male ego," Max drawled.

"Oh, yes. She's under the impression that as a staid, shy, humble professor of mathematics who's unaccustomed to dealing with situations such as this, you'd fall for it hook, line and sinker."

"May I ask what the point would be of leading on the staid, shy, humble professor?" Max's expression was one of unyielding granite.

"Now we come to the real beauty of Marcie's plan," Sophy said rather wearily. She had been up most of the previous night agonizing over Marcie's idea for revenge. The weariness she felt now was physical as well as mental. "While your male ego is thriving on my physical surrender, I am utilizing the opportunity to get close to you on every level."

"Marcie suggested some weird scheme whereby you allow me to think you're mine and then you betray me with another man, right?" he gritted.

"Nothing so primitive. Marcie Fremont is not a primitive sort of person. No, the idea was far more sophisticated than that. I'm to have my revenge on you by gaining access to the final version of the mathematical model you're doing for S & J Technology's new processing system. Once I have a copy of the model, I turn it over to Marcie."

Max looked blank. "Who will do what with it?"

"Who will then use it to exact her own revenge on S & J. She will use it to buy her way into a management position at a rival company. Marcie Fremont has given up waiting to have her abilities discovered and appreciated. She's going to find her own way to the top." Sophy closed her eyes and leaned her head back in the chair, remembering the incredible conversation with her friend. When she lifted her lashes again, she found Max staring at her in amazement.

"Oh, my God," he growled.

"Don't look so disgusted," Sophy advised. "Frankly, I think it might have worked."

"You're not making any of this up, are you?" he demanded incredulously.

"Nope. I have to admit my imagination is not that good."

There was a knock on the door, and with an irritated movement Max went to get the tray of tea. "Thanks," he muttered gruffly, hurriedly signing the tab and adding a tip. When he closed the door and turned back into the room, Sophy was reaching for her purse.

"Hold on, Sophy. You're not going anywhere just yet. Sit down." There was a new element of command in his voice, causing Sophy to blink warily. She hadn't heard that tone from him before.

"I've told you everything I know, Max."

"Why?"

"Why what?"

"Why did you tell me about Marcie's scheme? Why not simply go through with it?" He sat down again and watched her as if she were some infinitely complex formula he was trying to solve.

Sophy hesitated, unwilling to put into words the real reason she had been driven into coming to see Max. He was not to know that in the long hours of the preceding night she had battled with her own inability to exact a fitting revenge in such a manner. He was not to know that she had finally acknowledged at three o'clock in the morning that she could not bring herself to harm Max Travers in such a manner. If she stole the math model, he was bound to be implicated. He would be immediately suspect for having sold his work to a higher bidder. She had known with frightening clarity that she could not do that to Max Travers.

Her first loyalty had been to Max. But never would she admit that she was here tonight because she had discovered she felt strangely bound to this man.

"My parents might not have succeeded in drumming the principles of Einstein's theory of relativity into my head, but they did manage to teach me something about honorable conduct." It was as good an excuse as any.

"I see." Max appeared to be working out a problem. There was a preoccupied gleam in his eyes now.

"Look, Dr. Travers, I think this has gone far enough. I came here tonight to warn you because, frankly, I'm not sure I'm going to be able to stop Marcie. She's dead set on getting even with S & J Technology. To tell you the truth, I think she has a right to do exactly that. They treated her pretty shabbily. I think I can make her see reason eventually. She just needs a few days to cool down. In the meantime, I was afraid . . . I mean I thought she might . . ."

"You thought she might go through with the plan on her own somehow, right? So you decided to warn me, just in case." Max nodded, still looking thoughtful. "You're not interested in having your revenge, Sophy?" he finally asked.

She stiffened. "I'm not foolish enough to think there's

much chance of real revenge in a situation like this. This sort of thing has been happening to women since the dawn of time, and the victims rarely get a crack at getting even. Not if the victims, unlike the victors, have a sense of honor!"

She knew she'd gone too far with that last sentence. Sophy saw the grim fury in Max's eyes as she voiced the insult, and she badly wished she could recall the appalling words. In the tense moment that followed she fully expected to reap a whirlwind in retaliation. Her fingers clenched on the arms of her chair and her chin lifted in unconscious pride and defiance.

The effort Max made to control his anger was visible. What astonished Sophy was that he managed the feat. But when he spoke again his words were measured. "If the corporate-espionage bit was a little too extreme for you, I'm surprised you didn't consider the other alternative."

"What alternative?" she asked cautiously.

"The one I suggested. That of having an affair with me; leading me on and then betraying me with another man."

"And thoroughly cheapen myself in the process!"

"Having an affair with me would make you feel cheap?" Slowly Max got to his feet.

"Yes." Sophy eyed him uncertainly. It was time to leave, she realized, getting to her feet as well. The atmosphere in this hotel room had gone several points above the danger level.

But even as the realization struck her, Max's hands were coming down on her shoulders. "You're determined to play the wronged woman in all this, aren't you?" he bit out, giving her a small shake.

"I was wronged!"

"The hell with it. Since I'm already a condemned man in your eyes, I haven't anything left to lose, have I?" He dragged her against him, forcing her head back over his arm as he lowered his mouth to plunder her lips.

Sophy struggled wildly as his kiss claimed her. It was the other night all over again, but she didn't have the excuse this time of being in a state of emotional shock or even of having had too much to drink. How can it be like this? she raged helplessly as she felt her body leap to life. *It isn't fair!*

She hadn't realized she'd spoken her last thoughts aloud until Max muttered his response against her mouth.

"What you do to me isn't fair either. Sophy, Sophy, please don't fight me. Just let me have you. I need you." His hands moved down her back to her hips, shaping the full curve with hungry familiarity. "You can't walk away from what we had the other night. You can't expect me to walk away from it either."

Sophy wrenched her head to one side, trying to avoid his seeking mouth. "Max, you don't understand. I don't want this. I don't want a relationship based on physical attraction. I want a whole lot more than that. Why do you think I wouldn't go to bed with Nick?"

"For God's sake, don't talk to me about that damned cowboy! Not now!"

"I'm trying to make a point, darn you! I didn't go to bed with Nick because I was trying to build a relationship with him first. I have no intention of leading a life full of one-night stands!"

"The other night wasn't a one-night stand and you know it," he gritted, and then fastened his mouth on hers so that her next words were caught in her throat.

"Max, no . . ." she gasped when he finally pulled away.

"If you want a relationship, build one with me!"

"In the few days you'll be here in Dallas?" she mocked furiously. "That's hardly likely, is it? You can't build a meaningful relationship in a few days, and even if it were possible, you and I couldn't do it in a lifetime!"

"Why not?" he demanded flatly, holding her still as he lifted his head to stare down at her taut features.

"Because a relationship has to be based on such things as mutual respect, and there's no way on earth a man of your intellectual caliber is ever going to be able to respect my abilities. The most I'd ever be for you, Max, is a toy," she snapped. "And I won't play that role for any man."

His mouth curved into a faint hint of amusement for the first time. "Are you trying to tell me you want to be loved for your mind?"

The humor in him pushed her over the edge. It severed the careful rein she had on her temper. How dare he laugh at her on top of everything else? "Even the thought of such a thing makes you laugh, doesn't it?" she blazed up at him. "You insult me and then you have the nerve to wonder why I won't have an affair with you. Maybe you're not quite as bright as your academic achievements would indicate, Dr. Travers. Let me go!"

She stepped backward abruptly and his hands fell away, along with the amusement that had been edging his mouth. His eyes hardened.

"Sophy, stop it. You're behaving irrationally."

"Sometimes those of us at the lower end of the intelligence scale tend to function more on our emotions than on reason!"

"Then why don't you listen to your emotions?" he charged. "The way you did the other night when you gave yourself to me!"

"I'm not that big a fool!" she flung back harshly. Darn it, if she wasn't very careful she was going to burst into tears, and that must not be allowed to happen!

90

Yanking at the door handle, Sophy fled out into the hall. All she wanted to do now was escape. She needed to be free of the compelling influence this man had over her; needed to be free of the torment of her own emotions.

"Sophy, come back here. You can't go on running away from me!" He came after her, catching up to her at the elevators, his strong hands reaching out to halt her flight. She whirled angrily to face him.

"Let me go!"

"Not until you calm down."

"Someone's going to come along any minute and see you manhandling me in the hallway," she pointed out tautly. "Is that what you want?"

"What I want is a rational conversation!"

"Then you'll have to contact one of your academic colleagues. I don't have much talent in that area. Or any other area you're likely to be interested in either!"

At that his eyes became abruptly darker. "Now, that is an outright lie," he drawled. "You have a great deal of natural talent in bed."

She stared at him for an instant, utterly shattered by his wicked teasing, and then she lost her temper completely. Sophy slapped him. Not a ladylike tap on the cheek but a full-blown, arcing blow that had enough force behind it to snap his head to one side.

He didn't release her. When he looked back down at her there was warning in his gaze and his words were clipped. "I find your fiery temperament rather fascinating at times, but there are limits to how much of it I'll tolerate. Don't hit me again, Sophy."

"Or you'll hit me back?" she challenged. "I always said you were a real gentleman!"

Satisfied with the frustrated anger that leaped into his eyes, Sophy wrenched herself out of his grasp and stepped into the elevator as it arrived. Without a word she stared straight ahead as the doors closed. Only when he was safely out of sight and she realized she was alone in the elevator did Sophy relax her internal hold on her emotions. The tears began to trickle slowly down her cheeks.

Oh, God, what was the matter with her? How could she let him affect her this way? Half-blinded by the gleaming moisture in her eyes, she found her way through the huge lobby of the hotel and out into the parking lot. There, in the safety of her car, she gave way completely to the emotional storm that seemed to be raging inside her.

Eventually she managed to control the bout of tears and make her way home. It was Friday night. A week ago she would have looked forward to spending the evening with Nick Savage. Now every time she tried to think of Nick, the image of Max got in the way. She realized vaguely that she couldn't even summon up any anger toward Nick Savage now. All her emotions seemed to be focused on Max Travers.

Why a wizard? Why a man who lived in another world, an unreal world? A man who could never share her life, only her bed? Why did it have to be Max Travers who had succeeded in tapping the emotion that had lain dormant within her?

Sophy asked herself that question over and over again during the long drive home. She asked it as she morosely poured herself a glass of Chenin Blanc and settled down in her rainbow-hued chair to consider her life. She was still asking it an hour later when the telephone rang.

"Sophy? Don't hang up, this is important." Max's voice came across the wire with clipped command. "I've just been in touch with Graham Younger about what you told me this evening."

"Max! You didn't! I never meant for you to go to the president of the company!" Shocked, Sophy pulled herself out of her dismal reverie, her anxiety taking a sudden new twist. "I told you I'd handle Marcie."

"Sophy, have you told Marcie you aren't interested in her little scheme?"

"Well, no, not yet . . ." No sense trying to explain that she had been reluctant to confess to Marcie that she couldn't go through with it. "But I will!"

"No you won't."

"Says who?" she shot back angrily.

"Says your upper management. They've got plans."

"The hell they have!"

"We're to be in conference room number eighteen-oh-nine at eight o'clock tomorrow morning. S & J Security will be there to discuss the situation."

"Max! What have you done? I only warned you to be on the safe side. I never meant for you to drag management and Security into this!"

"You could hardly expect me to let a thing like this ride on your assumption that you can talk Marcie out of it! From what you told me and from what I've seen of her, she seems quite likely to go through with some sort of corporate espionage on her own, whether or not you get involved. She has to be stopped. S & J wants her neutralized."

"Neutralized! For God's sake! You don't know her the way I do. There is no need to take this kind of action. Max, why didn't you call me before you contacted Graham Younger? Why are you getting involved? Neutralizing would-be corporate espionage types is hardly your line of work. As long as you were warned, you could have taken a few precautions . . . ."

"Just show up in the conference room on time, all right?" he asked wearily.

"Wait a minute. Tomorrow is Saturday!" Desperately Sophy tried to think. She could hardly refuse to show up. Not if she wanted to keep her own job at S & J secure.

"Exactly. Security figures there won't be too many people around."

She needed time to work this out. And she couldn't afford to jeopardize her job. Sophy chewed on her lip. "All right, Max. It doesn't look like I have much choice. I'll be in tomorrow at eight."

"I'll see you there." Max hung up the phone before she had a chance to beat him to it.

Sophy sat glaring at the instrument for a long time before she roused herself to fix something for dinner. She had gotten so wrapped up in her own dangerously emotional response to Max that she had neglected to think about the implications of this whole mess for poor Marcie. Somehow warning Max had taken precedence. She hadn't stopped to consider what might happen if he dragged S & J management into it.

Not wanting to annoy the highest levels of corporate management, most of whom she had never met in person, Sophy arrived a little before eight the next morning and walked through the silent halls to the conference room. Though she was early, everyone else, it seemed, was there ahead of her.

Apparently S & J Technology had chosen to take the matter of Marcie Fremont very seriously. Sophy sighed and wondered what she'd unleashed as she greeted the president and his assistant very formally. Then she smiled at Sam Edison, the rather harried-looking man in the polyester suit who was in charge of S & J Security. She inclined her head very aloofly to Max, who had risen politely when she entered the room. Flustered by seeing someone in their midst rise to greet a mere secretary, the other males in the room had awkwardly done the same. Everyone sat down with relief.

"Miss Bennet," Graham Younger began pedantically,

"we certainly appreciate your willingness to cooperate with us in this matter."

As if I had any choice, Sophy thought, sliding a glance at Max's impassive face.

"It was very good of you to go straight to Dr. Travers with a report of the Fremont incident," he went on pompously. "You have brought to our attention a serious threat to this firm, Miss Bennet. Industrial and corporate espionage are major problems these days. As a company involved in high technology we are especially vulnerable. Therefore we are most anxious to nip Marcie Fremont's larcenous tendencies in the bud. We intend to make an example of her."

Sophy stared at the older man's implacable face, feeling suddenly chilled. Poor Marcie.

"Miss Fremont is only a secretary, of course," the president's assistant put in mildly, "but we feel we must make it clear that this sort of thing will not be dealt with lightly."

Only a secretary. The words were vastly annoying. "If you'll excuse me, sir," Sophy said coolly, "I think too much is being made of all this. I seriously doubt that any corporate espionage attempt will actually be made. Miss Fremont is not the sort to involve herself in that kind of thing. Miss Fremont is very professional."

"I'm afraid we can't take the chance," Sam Edison put in quickly. "We don't know who she might be working for."

"That's right, Miss Bennet," Younger said evenly. "Frankly, we don't believe Miss Fremont is working alone. This sort of sophisticated plot requires planning at much higher levels. We don't just want to stop her. We want to find out who she's working with and stop the entire espionage ring."

"Espionage ring! I don't think . . ." Sophy began earnestly.

"We're not asking for your opinion, Miss Bennet," Younger interrupted coolly. "You will be expected to give your full cooperation to our plan."

Sophy bit back her annoyance. "What plan?"

"As I understand it, Marcie Fremont seems to feel you, uh, have reason to be rather upset with Dr. Travers. A lovers' quarrel or something. You're supposedly motivated by revenge," Edison said quickly, obviously uncomfortable with the delicate matter.

Sophy's mouth fell open in amazement. Then her head swung around and she pinned Max with an infuriated glare. "You told him about . . . about . . ." Words dried up in her throat. The tide of her fury threatened to stifle her. Max had told S & J management that she wanted revenge because of a lovers' quarrel? She'd kill him! She'd slice him apart with her pinking shears!

"Calm down, Sophy," Max cut in sharply. "I explained that Marcie apparently misunderstood the situation between us and is trying to capitalize on it."

She stared at him. Everyone else in the room was looking distinctly uncomfortable, including Graham Younger. *They know,* she thought. *Max is going to answer for this!* Exerting her willpower to the utmost, she managed to bring her shaking fingers under control and bury them in her lap.

"What, exactly, do you want me to do, Mr. Edison?" she asked far too softly.

"Well, we, er, that is, if you'd pretend to go through with Miss Fremont's plan, we might be able to trace the flow of information. Dr. Travers will supply you with a phony version of the math model he's working on. You will pass it along to Miss Fremont and we'll be watching to see who she gives it to."

"Pretend to go through with Marcie's plan?" Sophy's eyes went to Max. He met her glare unflinchingly, but she could read nothing in his expression.

"Sophy," he said coolly, "I have explained to every-one in this room that you and I are not, uh, romantically involved and that Marcie simply misunderstood the situation. What Sam is asking is that you pretend to be involved with me and that you tell Marcie you're going through with the espionage scheme."

"There will, of course, be a bonus in it for you if the plan works," Graham Younger put in.

"I see." So, on top of everything else, they intended to buy her cooperation. Sophy had never felt so disgusted in her whole life. They were trying to trap her just as they intended to trap Marcie. And with the unlimited ego of the ruling elite of the business world, they assumed it would be a snap to manipulate two dumb little secretaries. Sophy let the heavy silence reign for a few minutes, refusing to surrender to the pressure. All of these males needed a lesson.

"I suppose you won't believe me if I tell you that you're all overreacting?" she finally murmured quietly.

"I think we're the best judges of the sort of reaction required in this instance, Miss Bennet," the president's assistant declared politely. "If you just concentrate on the bonus and on your duty to S & J Technology, we'll do the rest."

The bonus. Sophy smiled coldly. Let them think she was going to do it for the money. Let them think they could push Marcie and herself around. "Very well," she finally agreed. "I'll cooperate." There was a collective sigh of relief from everyone except Max, who eyed her warily but said nothing.

Sam Edison leaned forward, his elbows planted on the table, and intently began to explain their plan. The more he talked, the less she thought of it, but she let him babble on because she was busy making a few plans of her own.

An hour later she and Max both left the offices of S & J Technology, but they left separately.

"Meet me at the hotel," he ordered brusquely as he said goodbye.

"No more orders, Max." She faced him in the building lobby. "Is that very clear? We're suppposed to pretend to be lovers, but I won't go a step farther unless you agree to treat me as an equal partner in this stupid scheme."

"Sophy, I don't like this charade any better than you do, believe me!"

"I suppose there's nothing to do but make the best of it."

"Agreed. Now, how about lunch?" He sounded relieved.

"Lunch?"

"We are supposed to be spending the weekend together, remember? Part of the charade," he reminded her patiently. "I was wondering what plans you would like to make for lunch."

"Oh." She considered the matter and then said, "Actually, I did have some things to do today at home. Maybe dinner—"

"I'll bring some papers along and work on them while you're doing the things you wanted to do around your apartment," he interrupted. "We can have a sandwich or something for lunch. Doesn't have to be fancy."

For an instant Sophy thought she saw the jaws of a very lethal trap closing around her, and then she dismissed the image. She could handle Max Travers. As well as the management of S & J Technology.

Actually things might be easier if Max was busy working. She knew how totally involved people like him became when they were in the middle of a problem. She'd seen her parents disappear into their study for endless hours often enough. "All right, if that's what you would prefer."

"I'll get my briefcase from the hotel," he said before she could change her mind.

An hour later Sophy found that having Max in her kitchen was a strangely unsettling experience. He immediately adopted the kitchen table for a desk, appearing quite satisfied with the surroundings although they must have been much different from those in which he normally worked.

"What are you going to be doing this afternoon?" he asked as she opened the refrigerator to prepare sandwiches.

"I'm making a dress for one of the women at the office." Sophy found some cheese and a tomato and placed them on the counter. "Whole wheat bread or rye?"

"Rye please." He waited a moment and then said carefully, "That black dress you brought into the office the other morning looked rather nice."

She smiled cynically. "Thank you."

"Do you make your own clothes too?"

"Max, I know you're not really interested in discussing my sewing. Mustard or mayonnaise?"

"Both. What makes you say I'm not interested in your sewing?"

"Let me see if I can remember all the reasons why someone shouldn't take a hobby like sewing too seriously," she drawled, recalling her parents' lecture on the subject. "It's frivolous, takes up time that could better be spent on studying, and doesn't really engage the brain to any important extent."

"Whom are you quoting?" He half smiled, looking up from the table to watch her make the sandwiches.

"My mother and father. They were horrified when it became apparent that dress design wasn't going to be just a hobby for me but my main interest in life. They're going to be even more shocked when they find out I intend to open a design boutique here in Dallas." She slapped the cheese on the bread and sliced the tomatoes. When she turned to carry the sandwiches over to the table, she found Max smiling at her.

"It was hard on you, wasn't it, Sophy?" he asked quietly. "Growing up with two academically brilliant parents . . . ?"

"Who couldn't bring themselves to admit that they hadn't produced an equally brilliant child. Yeah, it was a little tough at times." She smiled wryly. "But I survived. And so did they."

"They love you."

"I know."

"You're lucky," he murmured.

She glanced up, frowning. "What do you mean?"

"Only that through all the trauma and the frustration, at least you knew you were loved."

"Meaning you weren't?"

"My parents were a lot like yours, Sophy. They wanted a child in their own image. But they were far too involved in their own careers to waste any time on loving me. They simply saw to it that I was given the best possible education. They apparently thought that was all that was necessary to raise a child."

She watched him uneasily. "You don't love your parents? They don't love you?"

"We can discuss higher math until three in the morning, and that's generally what we talk about when I visit. But that's about all we do together. When I was a kid I remember several Christmases when we didn't even have a tree because my parents were so busy with their studies and their research that they just forgot to get one. When they remembered presents they were always the educational variety."

"No crayons?" she asked with a smile.

"No crayons. Or anything else that was just plain fun."

Sophy felt a tide of compassion for the little boy who had been programmed to be a genius and who was never allowed to deviate from the program. Firmly she squelched the sensation. Damn it, she was not going to allow this man to play on her sympathy.

"You don't trust me, do you, Sophy?" he asked.

"Would you in my place?" she countered.

Unexpectedly he smiled. "You could try seducing me and we could find out what my reaction would be. I think I'd trust you afterward."

"Forget it." She got to her feet and picked up her dish. "Do you want ribs or a steak tonight? I'd better get them out of the freezer now so they'll be ready to barbecue later."

"A steak sounds fine."

"Okay." She reached into the freezer and dragged out a package. "I'll look forward to seeing you earn your keep tonight."

"What's that mean?"

She glanced up ingenuously. "I'll look forward to watching you grill the steak tonight," she clarified politely.

Max's mouth lifted wryly. "Sorry, you're out of luck. My domestic skills are limited to opening cans and sticking frozen dinners in microwave ovens."

Sophy's sense of humor rose to the surface. Exactly as she had suspected. "Another gap in your education. You can't type and you can't barbecue. Well, Max, prepare yourself. You're in Texas now, and here in Texas every real man knows how to grill a steak."

"Now, wait a minute, Sophy . . ."

"No excuses are necessary. Tonight, Max, you're going to cook a steak. Consider it an extension of your education."

6

When she emerged from her elaborately outfitted sewing room later that afternoon, Sophy smelled smoke. Curious, she followed the scent through the kitchen, where Max's paper work was neatly stacked on the table, and out onto the patio. There she found Max, white shirt smudged with charcoal, eyeing the small flame he had produced in the pit of the barbecue grill.

"You look as if you're going to be forced to walk across the coals in your bare feet," she teased as he continued to stare at the charcoal with deep suspicion.

"Sophy, I told you I don't know much about this sort of thing," he growled.

"What good is a man who can't barbecue a steak?" she asked flippantly. "I'll go see about the salad. Women's work, you know." With a small sense of triumph that she knew was really very childish, Sophy went back inside the kitchen. He was going to ruin the steak, of course. It was a small thing, but he was going to make a fool out of himself in front of her and the thought brought some satisfaction. Well worth the price she had paid for the meat.

From time to time as she went about the business of preparing the salad and warming crusty rolls, she glanced surreptitiously out the window to watch Max. He was deep in concentration, intently studying the few instructions printed on the back of the package of charcoal briquettes. Sophy laughed to herself, relishing the moment when he would actually have to put the meat on the fire. She just hoped he realized that he was supposed to put it on the grill and not directly in the flames!

He was getting anxious, she thought as she came and went on the patio, setting the small, glass-topped wicker table and arranging the salad dishes.

"About ready for the steak?" she asked brightly.

Max looked up from his intent contemplation of the coals and started to say something. Whatever it was, he changed his mind at the last moment and nodded brusquely. Sophy smiled serenely and went back inside to get the meat.

"A pity to sacrifice a good piece of steak," she muttered to herself as she hoisted the tray and carried it out to Max with a flourish. "But it is going to be interesting to see just how burnt the offering is before he elects to serve it to me."

Max's gaze narrowed as he watched her approach with the meat. "Sophy, are you sure you don't want to take over?"

"Nonsense. Any man can grill a steak. It's an instinct, I believe. Every man I've ever known could handle a barbecue. Except my father, of course," she added blandly. "And I guess, now that I think about it, there were a few other exceptions. Mostly academic exceptions. Let me rephrase my original statement. Every man I've ever *dated* could handle a barbecue and a steak."

"In other words, you don't date men who can't project the machismo image, is that it?" he gritted, practically yanking the glass tray out of her hands. "Should I buy a horse and start wearing a six-gun?"

"I wouldn't bother going to the expense, if I were you. After all, you'll only be in town a short while, remember? I'll fix you a drink. Men usually sip a whiskey or something while they're grilling a steak."

"Actually," he retorted, carefully unwrapping the steak from its plastic covering, "that sounds like one of your better ideas."

Sophy grinned again and went back inside to fix the drinks. After handing him his, she sank down onto the nearest patio chair, propped up her feet and prepared to witness the debacle. Max had already thrown the meat on the grill. Much too soon, she thought critically. It was going to be charred on the outside and raw on the inside.

"I'll tell Marcie that I'm going along with her big plan on Monday morning," Sophy said conversationally. "How long shall we wait before I turn over the fake information?" No sense telling Max she had other plans for S & J.

Max didn't look up from the burning steak. "A week, maybe. We can't rush it any more than that or she'll be suspicious."

"If she's as smart as I think she is she'll be suspicious anyway. Honestly, this has got to be the craziest scheme I've ever heard. Hard to believe it came from a man of Graham Younger's stature."

"Don't forget that the head of Security thinks it will work, too."

Sophy shook her head in disgust. "Let's drop it, Max."

"What would you like to talk about?" he asked evenly.

She lifted one shoulder negligently. "Anything but higher mathematics."

"How about your plans to open a design boutique?" he surprised her by suggesting.

She watched him through half-concealing lashes. "Are you sure you're interested in my plans?"

"Sophy, anything that you're involved in interests me," he said simply.

She hesitated. "Okay, but don't blame me if you get bored quickly."

"The one thing I never am around you is bored." He gave her a fleeting smile. "I think you're my missing crayons."

"Your what?"

"The crayons I never had a chance to play with as a child. Life has always been rather black-and-white for me, Sophy. You're like a rainbow in it."

Sophy stared at him, uncertain how to take the gentle confession. He was doing it again, she thought, making her feel sorry for him, eliciting her compassion. She was going to have to be extremely careful around this man. He was proving to be dangerous in ways she would never have expected.

"Well, pay attention," she ordered gruffly. "My folks will want to know all the shocking details of my decision to make my dress designing into a career." And while he finished massacring the steak, she told him about her plans for the future.

"Designing and sewing for people has been a sideline for me since college, but it's only been during the past year that I've actually considered making a full-time career out of it," she concluded. "Dallas, with its optimistic, adventurous, anybody-can-get-rich-here atmosphere, seemed like a good place to try my luck.

That bonus Younger promised me this morning might make the difference between my being able to take the plunge a few months from now or a year from now." Except that she never intended to collect that bonus!

"Is that the real reason you agreed to go along with the plan? The bonus?" Clearly he was remembering her comment about Marcie's threat to his career.

"Let's just say it was an excellent incentive," she murmured, not wanting to discuss the issue. The truth was, she realized unhappily, if Max hadn't been threatened along with S & J, she might have been tempted to let the company take its chances. It might teach management a good lesson if it got ripped off by a "mere" secretary! Now she had to concoct a more involved scheme to show Graham Younger the error of his ways.

Max stared down at the incinerated steak, and she sensed the wary anxiety he was feeling about the meat's condition. "I guess if we're ever going to eat, it might as well be now," he said.

"Lovely," she drawled smoothly, rising to her feet. "I'll get the wine."

The steak was charred almost beyond recognition. In a land where everyone preferred his meat rare, it was a total disaster. Oh, there was a rare, almost raw section left in the center, Sophy noted as she cut into her piece, but it looked quite unappetizing surrounded by the overdone part. There was little if any natural juice left in the meat. Max had stabbed the poor thing so many times with his cooking fork that it had all drained out. Dry, charred and tough, the steak was as thoroughly ruined as it was possible for a piece of meat to be. Sophy should have been feeling a sense of triumph.

After all, Max was clearly feeling as nervous and awkward about his failure at the barbecue as she would have felt trying to work a problem in one of his math classes. It was a small thing, but Sophy told herself she was giving him a taste of being a failure. Served him right. As she took the first bite she considered exactly how she would show her disdain for his inability to cope with such an elementary task.

Then she glanced up and found him watching her with nervous dread apparent in his gray eyes. He was waiting for the axe to fall, she realized abruptly. He knew as well as she did that the meat was terrible, and he undoubtedly knew exactly what she was going to say. There was a grim, stoically resigned expression on his hard features. He hadn't held his own against the men he was being measured against and he knew it. He'd probably known from the beginning that he didn't stand a chance. What hope did he have, never having grilled a steak before in his life?

Sophy read the reaction in him and told herself it was all she could have wished. Now was the time for a cold, cutting remark and a few choice, derogatory comments on his failure as a chef. It wasn't much, but it might be all the revenge she ever got. In some small way she had a chance to show Max Travers that as far as she was concerned, he was a nonstarter in her world.

"It's delicious," she heard herself say as she chewed with polite greed. "Exactly the way I like it. Honestly, everyone here in Texas insists on serving it so raw that it bleeds all over the plate. I've been too embarrassed to tell anyone that I like my meat well-done."

He stared at her, plainly astonished. He wasn't the only one, Sophy decided ruefully; she was equally startled at her words. But she knew she wasn't going to retract them. Instead she gave him a genuine smile and passed the glass salad bowl. What in the world was the matter with her?

Taking it automatically from her hands, Max continued to survey her intently. "You like it?" he finally managed.

"Ummm. I guess you have a natural talent for the barbecue, after all. Would you like some steak sauce?" She was pouring a lot over her own meat. It might help.

"Yes, thank you," he murmured humbly. Then he visibly began to relax. "I was a little uncertain about the timing," he confessed, picking up his own knife and fork. "You're sure you like it well-done?"

"My favorite way," Sophy assured him cheerfully.

He took his first bite and chewed steadily for a long moment. "Don't you think it's a little tough?" he asked diffidently.

"That's the fault of the meat, not you." She smiled. "It was a cheap cut. They usually turn out tough on the grill." Actually, she'd paid a fortune for it.

"Oh." He nodded wisely, apparently relieved.

"I probably should have served the ribs, but I wanted to use up this beef. It's been in the freezer quite a while." Another lie. Why?

"It's not very juicy," he said tentatively, obviously appealing for more reassurance.

"That's because it spent so long in the freezer," she lied gamely. "Have a little more steak sauce on it."

Max appeared to relax even further. "Maybe we should have marinated this steak beforehand," he said very knowledgeably.

Sophy stifled a laugh. All the marinating in the world would not have compensated for the way it was treated on the grill. "You're probably right. Next time I have an old, cheap cut of beef, I'll try marinating it first. You did an excellent job with what you had to work with, Max. Delicious."

Why, she asked herself anxiously, was she bothering to pretend Max had acquitted himself well at the barbecue? Why hadn't she seized her small moment of triumph? What on earth had made her compliment him on the ruined meat just as though he were a man she really cared about, a male whose ego she wanted to soothe?

Damn it! This was the man who had deliberately taken advantage of her, and here she was comforting and reassuring him! She must be out of her mind.

By the end of the meal, Max was showing signs of reacting to his success at the barbecue the way men always react to their triumphs. He was pleased with himself, jovial, willing to talk about anything and everyone. A man on top of the world. Sophy didn't know whether to laugh or cry. It occurred to her that she might have created a monster.

"Next time I think I'll experiment a bit with the coals," he informed her seriously. "I think it might be a good idea to let them die down a little first before putting on the meat. What do you think?"

"Possibly," she agreed cautiously. "I'm really not much of an expert on barbecues."

"Because you always leave that side of things to the men in your life?" He smiled wryly. "Well, now that I'm the only man in your life, you won't have to worry about whether or not your next date can grill a steak, will you?"

Sophy looked at him helplessly. She *had* created a monster. "Are you as good at washing dishes as you are at barbecuing?"

"Better. I've had more practice in that department. Been a bachelor for thirty-six years, you know. I've washed a lot of dishes in my time."

"That may be more of an asset in the long run than being accomplished at the barbecue," she said lightly, rising to begin clearing the table. "A lot of women would value that talent more than barbecuing skill!"

"How about you, Sophy?"

"I've got a dishwasher," she informed him sweetly.

"Good thing I passed the test at the barbecue grill,

then, isn't it?" he drawled softly behind her. "Since my other skills don't count with you?"

"Would you like some dessert, Max?" Determinedly, she started toward the kitchen with a stack of dishes. Damned if she was going to let him drag her any deeper into the quagmire that seemed to be stretching at her feet.

"Sure. What have you got?"

"Ice cream?"

"I can prepare ice cream even better than I can grill a steak," he confided cheerfully, opening the freezer and searching out the carton of chocolate ice cream she had inside.

What was she going to do with him this evening? Sophy wondered a little nervously. He was settling in very thoroughly. Very soon now she was going to have to make it quite clear that she had no intention of playing out Graham Younger's charade to the extent of allowing him to spend the night. Sophy began to feel trapped by the complex web of circumstances. She must perform this balancing act very carefully or face disaster.

She was lecturing herself on that point when the doorbell rang imperiously. "Now what? One more problem is all I need."

Max glanced up from his task of shoveling out huge scoops of chocolate ice cream. "What did you say?"

"I said, there's the doorbell," she lied politely, wiping her hands on a towel and walking into the living room to answer it. Who could it be on Saturday night? If it was Sam Edison or someone from S & J Technology checking up on her, she would be furious. On the other hand, what if it was Marcie Fremont?

Sophy opened the door with a frown and found all six feet, three inches of Nick Savage standing there. She stared at his handsome face in utter shock.

"You were the last person I expected to see here

tonight," she informed him starkly. "What the hell do you want?"

"You," he said with devastating simplicity. He pushed the Stetson back on his head and his eyes gleamed down at her. "I figured I'd given you long enough to get over your little temper tantrum. I've missed you, darlin'."

Sophy was incredulous. "You've *missed* me! What an idiotic thing to say! The last time I saw you, you had plenty of company, as I recall. Go visit your blond girlfriend if you're lonely this evening."

Nick put out a hand and tousled her curls in the old, familiar manner. "You know, you're kinda cute when you're mad, honey. Now stop glaring at me and I'll explain all about Trisha."

"If Trisha is the blond, I'd just as soon not hear all the details."

"Honey," he drawled, "Trisha was just a way of fillin' time until you were willing to let me into your bed. She means nothin' to me. She's just a good-time girl."

"Well, go have a good time with her. You're not going to have one with me, I guarantee!" she hissed.

"Now, you don't mean that and you know it." He smiled confidently. "You're just a little upset because you caught me foolin' around with Trisha. I wouldn't have been, you know, if you'd kept our date that night."

"How dare you make it sound as if it were all my fault! You've probably been playing around with her all the time I've known you!"

"Like I said, honey, I was just fillin' in time—"

"Oh, shut up, Nick, and leave. I'm really not interested in discussing this further."

"Now, that's where you're wrong, darlin'. We both know you're very interested in discussing this. You're in love with me, remember?" His voice was smooth and assured. Nick was very sure of himself, Sophy realized.

"You really believe you can just walk back in like this and everything will be all right?" she whispered scathingly.

"I know you're a little upset about Trisha . . ."

Sophy shook her head. "Oh, Nick, you don't even have an inkling, do you?"

"I've got more than an inkling of how you feel about me," he murmured, stepping through the door. "You might be mad as hell about that little scene by the pool, but you'll get over it. With some help."

On the last words, he hauled her into his arms and lowered his head to find her mouth. Sophy stood perfectly still, deciding that the quickest way to discourage him was to show him that he couldn't influence her now with his casually expert lovemaking.

Even though she had no intention of betraying any reaction, it still came as something of a surprise to Sophy to find she *had* no reaction. Where was the pleasant warmth she had once experienced in Nick's arms? Why wasn't she responding even a little to the sensuous expertise he wielded so well?

Sophy was still working that one out when Max Travers's voice cut through the air like an uncoiling whip.

"Take your hands off her, Savage, or I'll stuff that Stetson hat down your throat!"

Sophy jumped, as much from the shock of hearing such violence in Max's tone as from his unexpected interruption. "Max!" She tried to push herself away from a grim-faced Nick, but he reached out to hold her, his arm gripping her shoulders. They both stared at Max, who was standing in the kitchen doorway with the carton of ice cream still in one hand.

"Who the hell is this?" Nick asked in astonishment, clearly not seeing any threat in the man who was challenging him.

"I'm the man who took her to bed the night you had

your private little poolside party with the blond. Remember me? I was standing right behind Sophy when you came out of the cabana. I took her to my hotel after the show."

"Max! Please!" Sophy felt anger and fear rising up and twisting together in her stomach. She was angry at Max for his blatant claim on her, and she was afraid for him—afraid that Nick Savage would tear him apart. Already she could feel the fighting tension in Nick's body. The arm locked around her shoulders tightened.

"I don't believe you," Nick said dangerously. He sent a disdainful glance over Max. "You're not exactly her type."

"Maybe not," Max agreed easily. "But she's my type. Ask her. Ask her if she didn't spend the night with me. Ask her if she didn't give herself to me completely that night. *Go ahead! Ask her!*"

"What the hell's he talkin' about, Sophy?" Nick didn't look down at her, his whole attention on Max, whom he clearly couldn't imagine as real competition.

"He's just trying to be protective," Sophy said hurriedly, pulling free of Nick's grip. "He saw you that night by the pool and he's trying to protect me from you!" It was all she could think of at the moment. Damned if she was going to stand there and admit Max was telling the truth! The bastard! When this was over she'd give him a piece of her mind.

"I see," Nick said coolly. "Well, there's no call to play Sir Galahad. The little lady and I can work this out for ourselves. We don't need your interference. Why don't you run along and finish eating your ice cream? On second thought, why don't you just leave altogether? I don't much like the idea of Sophy here entertaining other men in the evening, even if they do let her cry on their shoulders."

Sophy caught her breath as Max slowly put down the carton of ice cream and removed his glasses. Automatically he began polishing them on his shirt. "I'm not going anywhere, Savage. You're the one who will have to leave." He held the frames up to the light, squinting to check the polishing job. "Tell him, Sophy."

"Tell him what?" she snapped, enraged and genuinely frightened now. If Max didn't stop goading Nick there would be hell to pay. On the other hand, she told herself a little violently, maybe Max deserved to find himself flat on the floor.

"Tell him you're mine now. That you've spent a night in my bed and that you'll probably spend tonight with me too." He replaced the glasses with great care.

"Not tonight, too!" she shouted, and realized too late it was the wrong thing to deny. She should have denied spending the first night with him. Nick's narrowed eyes swung to her instantly.

"Sophy?" he began with soft menace, and for the first time Sophy realized just how dangerous the situation really was. She summoned her poise and faced him as coolly as possible.

"I think you'd better leave, Nick."

"Why, you little bitch!" he snarled. "It's true, isn't it? You actually went to bed with this little nerd, didn't you? Of all the cheatin', lyin', little bitches!" His hand came around so fast, so unexpectedly, that Sophy didn't even have a chance to avoid it. Nick struck the side of her face in a flat, vicious slap that sent her sprawling to the floor. She was too stunned even to cry out.

Before she could gather her senses, the room seemed to explode around her. She saw Max's nearly silent rush across the jade green carpet and cried out. "Max, no! He'll kill you!"

But neither man paid her the slightest attention. The atmosphere in the room had gone very primitive in a hurry, Sophy realized, terrified. She struggled to a sitting position, her palm on her sore cheek, and watched in horror as Nick closed with Max.

The police! If she could just get to the phone . . . Sophy tried to rise to her knees and succeeded in doing so just as Nick landed with a thud on the carpet beside her. Eyes wide with shock, she knelt, looking down at him. Then she glanced up at Max, who was calmly brushing off his sleeve.

"Are you ready to leave yet, Savage?" Max asked quietly.

"I'm gonna kill you, you bastard!" Nick gritted, getting to his feet and launching himself at Max in a low, powerful rush.

The results were the same as before. Max did something very economical and smooth with his hands and Nick landed once again flat on his back. This time he didn't get up quite so quickly. Max stood calmly waiting for him.

"You think 'cause you got lucky a couple of times I can't take you?" Nick muttered furiously. "Well, you're wrong. I'm gonna take you apart limb from limb!"

Max easily sidestepped the next bull-like rush, slicing down with his hand as Nick flew past. Like a matador in a ring, he toppled the other man with a seemingly casual display of skill. This time Nick didn't rise at all. He simply lay groaning on the floor. Sophy watched, half-numb with shock, as Max went over to his fallen victim and crouched beside him.

"Come near her again, Savage, and I'll do a lot more damage. She's mine now and she stays mine. You don't want her, anyway, remember? You threw away your chances with Sophy the night you screwed that little blond by the pool. You're a fool, but that's not my problem. Go find yourself another little blond."

Nick glowered up at him, massaging his arm. "I'll get you for this!"

Max raised one eyebrow. "Why bother? Would you really want her back? Knowing she gave herself to me so easily after refusing you for months?"

Nick's angry glare swung back to where Sophy still knelt on the carpet. "Cheatin' little bitch. Nah, I don't want her," he spat. "You can have her!" He rolled to his feet and lurched furiously for the door. Max rose slowly, his eyes never leaving his opponent. On the threshold, Nick turned to stare briefly at him. "I guess you won her fair and square, nerd, but take some advice. Don't let her string you along the way she did me. Made a damn fool out of me, putin' me off while she decided how she really felt! Led me a real dance, she did."

"While you were busy dancing with someone else?" Max half smiled.

"Man's got a right to some action on the side," Nick grunted huffily.

"Goodbye, Savage." Max waited for the other man to leave. Neither male glanced at Sophy, who was beginning to feel like a doe during mating season. Never in her life had she had a fight conducted over her, and the experience was the most primitive and unpleasant she had ever been through.

Without another word Nick slammed the door behind him and stalked down the path toward the waiting Lincoln. It wasn't until they heard the muted roar of the powerful engine that Max turned slowly to confront Sophy.

In absolute silence they regarded each other across the room. Sophy felt a combination of wariness and relief that left her trembling. Slowly she staggered to her feet, clutching at the nearest chair for support. She didn't like the glinting, fundamentally male expression in Max's smoky gray eyes.

"Max?" she began uneasily.

"I think," Max said slowly, "that the dumb cowboy may have had a point." He started toward her with an even, purposeful pace. "I did win you fair and square, didn't I? And I would be a fool to let you string me along, wouldn't I? You belong to me now."

"Max, stop it!" she whispered, backing away carefully as he approached. "I mean it. Stop it."

"I just fought a knock-down, drag-out battle for you, lady. I've never fought over a woman in my life."

"Max, this has gone far enough. I won't have any more violence in this house!" She backed away another step, chilled at the implacable look on his face.

"No," he agreed. "No violence."

"I'll call the police!"

"Not just now." He spoke almost absently as he came to a halt a foot away from her and lifted a hand to touch the cheek Nick had struck. "If he ever tries to hit you again I'll kill him."

Sophy shivered as he possessively smoothed her cheek. Her eyes never left his face. She could feel the male aggression flowing from him, a by-product of the fight, no doubt. And she knew before he said another word that she was going to be the target of that aggression.

"You belong to me," he repeated in a soft, rasping voice. "I just won you fair and square." He pulled her into his arms.

7

The unfathomable, unnerving, incomprehensible part was that a part of Sophy agreed with him. She was shaken, overwhelmed by the violence that had just taken place. She was equally unsettled by the knowledge that, having lain once in Max Travers's arms, she no longer felt anything when Nick Savage kissed her. What had this wizard done to her?

She couldn't seem to think logically as his mouth descended to claim hers. Sophy tried to tell herself that she shouldn't be responding so unreservedly to Max's compelling hold, but her lips parted in surrender beneath his and she knew the truth. She was deeply attracted to this man and she wanted him. In some distant corner of her mind she even acknowledged that the attraction went far beyond anything she had ever known—perilously close to love. Oh, no! She must not be in love with him!

He was all wrong for her! But even as the lecture rang

through her brain, Sophy heard a soft moan and knew it came from her own throat.

"I want you, sweetheart," Max grated as he teased her mouth with his own.

"Oh, Max . . ."

"I'm going to take you tonight," he muttered, pulling away to look down at her flushed face with burning eyes. His hands moved compellingly along the length of her spine, finding the nerves at the bottom of it and kneading sensually. "I'm going to strip all these bright clothes from your beautiful body and find the rainbow underneath. And then I'm going to make love to the rainbow. Oh, God, Sophy, don't try to stop me. Nothing could stop me now. I need you too much."

She trembled in his embrace, knowing that she wouldn't stop him even if she could. "Wizard," she whispered, burying her face against his shoulder.

She knew he sensed the surrender in her. She could feel the triumph and satisfaction in him, yet at the same time his hands on her were tender. Locked against the length of his body by one of his arms, Sophy felt him fumbling with the fastenings of her clothes. His fingers trembled slightly with the force of his desire, but they didn't hesitate. The colorful cotton knit skirt and top were lying in a pool at her feet before Sophy was fully aware of what had happened.

"You have skin like silk." Max brushed his lips along her shoulder while he undid the clasp of her small bra. When the garment fell away, he groaned and curved his palms wonderingly around her breasts. "I love the feel of your nipples when they get hard under my hands. Like small, ripe berries."

His hands slid to her waist, lifting her up with an easy strength. When her breasts were level with his mouth, he nipped erotically at both before lowering her down along the length of his body. Sophy shivered and whispered his name.

"Put your arms around my neck and hold on to me while I get undressed," he ordered thickly. Obediently she did as she was told, twining her arms around him. She met his steady, fiercely glowing gaze as he unbuttoned his shirt and unfastened his belt buckle. A moment later his clothes, too, lay on the floor, and he stood fully naked in front of her.

Deliberately he reached up to catch hold of her wrists, drawing her hands down over his shoulders, across his chest and along the firm, taut line of his stomach. Then he bent his head and plunged his tongue deeply into her mouth as he pushed her hands down further to the throbbing evidence of his desire.

Sophy gasped at the bold demand, but the masculine aggression in him brooked no denial. With delicate fingers she found the waiting hardness and gently caressed.

"Sophy," he groaned into her mouth, "Sophy, your touch is enough to send me out of my mind!" He deepened the kiss and slid his hands around to clench the curve of her buttocks. When Sophy gasped again, he slipped his palms inside the nylon panties she still wore and found the secret hidden in the triangle of tightly curling hair. Impatiently he pushed the panties off altogether.

"Oh, Max!"

"I can feel the heat in you, sweetheart," he groaned as he began to stroke magic patterns on the heart of her desire. "So warm and welcoming. Put your arms back around my neck."

"But, Max . . ." She wanted to go on touching him, exciting him. Arousing a wizard was heady business.

"Do as I say, my sweet love," he urged. When she once again had her hands locked around his neck, he pushed his bare foot between her legs, gently forcing her to stand with her feet apart.

Sophy was suddenly aware of feeling incredibly,

sensuously vulnerable. Too vulnerable. Instinctively she started to lower her hands, but he stopped her with a muttered word and a reassuring kiss. She trembled as he began to caress her more intimately, his fingers boldly invading her body.

"I want to know I can make you want me," he growled huskily as his hand stoked the fire in her. "I want to feel you trembling and hear the soft sounds you make when you're aroused. I want you to know just how much you want me, too. Tell me, Sophy. Tell me with words as well as with your body!"

Her head fell back as she looked up into his passion-carved face. How could she deny this wizard anything he asked tonight? She belonged to him. He had fought for her and now he seemed to have every right to seduce her. God help her, she was feeling every bit as primitive as he was.

"Max, I want you. You must know I want you," she got out in a throaty little voice.

"Did you ever want that damn cowboy this much? Did your body become hot and damp and did you tremble when he touched you?"

"No," she gasped as he did something unbelievable to the center of her. "No, never like this. It was never like this with him. . . . It's never been like this with anyone," she added helplessly as she moved against his hand. "Please, Max, please make love to me. . . ."

"I am making love to you," he drawled gently.

"You know what I mean." Urgently she writhed, forcing her hips closer to his.

"What do you mean, Sophy?" he growled. "Tell me exactly what you mean."

"Take me," she begged. "Here. Now. Please take me." She used her hands on his neck, trying to make him sink to the carpet with her. Slowly he followed her as she went down to her knees.

"You're sure this is what you want?" he taunted.

"Don't tease me, Max!" Sophy went down onto her back, pulling him urgently across her body.

"I only take what's mine," he warned deeply.

"I am yours," she cried, opening her thighs for him. "Oh, Max, I *am* yours. I belong to you."

"Fair and square," he murmured hoarsely, and then he was completing the union with a rush of power and strength that momentarily deprived her of breath.

Sophy gave herself up joyously to the passionate wizardry of the man who was claiming her body so completely. There might be a price to pay later, but tonight everything seemed right. There was no alternative tonight other than to succumb to this thrilling torture.

The overwhelming excitement seemed to twist tighter and tighter within her until Sophy thought she would break apart into a thousand glittering pieces. Max seemed to understand every nuance of the sensations that assaulted her, and he capitalized on each one. His body drove relentlessly into hers, mastering, taking, leading and guiding. She could do nothing but cling to him, her legs wrapped around his waist, her arms clutching at his shoulders.

Higher and higher they raced until the final twisting convulsion claimed Sophy completely.

"Oh, my God, *Max!*"

"Yes, darling, yes," he ground in her ear, nipping savagely. "Hold on to me and let yourself go."

Her throat arched and her eyes were tightly shut as Sophy let the tide of passion sweep through her. She was dimly aware of an exultant masculine cry and felt Max's body go rigid in the final response. Then she was drifting, catching her breath and marveling at the utter relaxation of her body.

When she gradually surfaced a long time later it was to find Max still lying along the length of her, his legs tangled with her own. She opened her eyes to find him balanced on his elbows, looking down into her face. For a moment they stared at each other.

It was Max who broke the spell of bemusement. "If someone had told me two weeks ago that I would take advantage of a woman and seduce her and then fight some cigarette-ad cowboy for her and follow that up with another seduction, I would have told him to go play with an abacus. Sophy, you bring out a side of me I never knew existed." He looked dazzled and stunned by his own actions.

She lifted a hand to play with the hair at the back of his damp neck. "And if anyone had told me I'd be seduced by a wizard, I would have said he was crazy. Max, what have you done to me?" she whispered, dazed.

"Made you mine." He dipped his head and feathered a kiss along the top of her breast. Then he licked the glistening perspiration that had collected in the hollow between the two soft globes. "And I'm going to go on making you mine again and again until you finally believe it yourself. I want you to know it for a fact, not just when I've got you lying under me like this, but every waking moment of your life."

She didn't know what to say—didn't really want to say anything. It was all too frightening and dangerous to consider closely. Her instincts bid her flee and her body said that was impossible. When she stayed silent, her blue-green eyes wide and eloquent, his mouth kicked upward in wry amusement and he kissed her gently. "Don't fight me, Sophy. I want you so, and I can't resist reaching out to take you."

Her lashes lowered as Sophy realized she couldn't maintain direct contact with his eyes. She licked her lips tentatively, aware of the swollen feel of them. Her whole body felt the vivid aftermath of passion. "Max, why didn't Nick beat you to a pulp?"

"You thought he was going to, didn't you?" he

retorted whimsically. "You were afraid for me, weren't you?"

"Yes." It was the truth. She had been terrified that Nick would hurt him badly.

"I like having you worried about me," Max decided.

"But how did you handle him so easily? It was like watching a matador and a rather awkward bull. You didn't even get your shirt rumpled."

He grinned, a wicked, utterly masculine grin that told her just how pleased he was with himself. The triumphant male. "Right," he stated categorically, "was on my side."

"Uh-huh. Along with a little scientific judo?"

"Hapkido," he corrected. "I work out with a colleague of mine who's an expert." He lost interest in the matter, beginning to toy with the crown of her breast. "You make me feel so unbelievably fantastic, Sophy. I would have fought ten clones of that cowboy tonight for the right to possess you." Before she could say anything he suddenly came alert.

"What's wrong?"

"The ice cream! I just remembered I left it sitting on that table over there. It's going to be melting all over the place." He got to his feet in a lithe movement and strode across the room to collect the rapidly softening ice cream. At the doorway into the kitchen he turned and glared at her. "Don't move. I'll be right back."

Sophy stayed where she was, not at all certain she could move. Her body felt boneless, utterly satiated. Her mind was in a shifting, dreamy state that was new to her. She had no will to look beyond the present. It was far easier to focus only on this moment. Sophy was still telling herself that when she realized Max was standing beside her.

"Now you can get up," he murmured, reaching down to lift her to her feet.

She opened her eyes and drew in her breath at the

arrogant maleness of him. Every inch of his body seemed to tug at her senses. The musky scent of him was intoxicating. When she came to her feet in front of him, she stumbled as her legs refused to function properly.

"Poor Sophy," he whispered, sounding quite satisfied with her unsteady condition. "You're not sure yet what's happened to you, are you?" He bent and lifted her easily into his arms and smiled as the curling mane of her hair tumbled across his shoulder.

"Where . . . where are we going?" Not that she would be able to protest if she didn't like the destination, Sophy decided with an inner smile. She was too enthralled by Max's wizardry tonight to do anything else except stay with him.

"To bed."

She leaned her head against his shoulder, her fingers playing idly with the fascinating cloud of hair on his chest, and let herself be carried down the hall to the bedroom. There in the darkness he settled her gently onto turned-down sheets. Then he stood for a moment, drinking in the sight of her lying in the center of the bed, waiting for him. Sophy could read the exultant arousal that was beginning anew in his eyes. Wordlessly she opened her arms.

"Sophy, you make my blood sing." Then he was lowering himself to her once more, gathering her close. All through the endless night Sophy stayed safely locked in the wizard's possessive embrace. She refused to think about the coming dawn.

Ultimately, it wasn't the dawn that awakened her the next morning. It was the ringing of the telephone. Sophy came drowsily to her senses, aware that the bed was empty beside her and aware, too, of the fragrance of freshly made coffee.

The phone rang again. There was something about the phone in the mornings, she reminded herself vaguely. Something about the phone ringing on Sunday mornings. Was it Sunday? Her mother always called on Sunday mornings. With a start, Sophy struggled to a sitting position and reached for the extension beside the bed.

Before she could pick it up she heard Max answer on the living room extension. Helplessly Sophy listened to his greeting. She prayed that it was not her mother.

"Hello? No, you've got the right number. This is Sophy Bennet's apartment. What? Who's this? This is Max Travers speaking. Why, hello, Dr. Bennet. Good to talk to you again. How's the weather back there? Hotter 'n' hell down here in Texas. You were right about Dallas, by the way, all chrome and glass and western atmosphere. Did you know they've still got real live cowboys left down here? Not as tough as they used to be. Then again, maybe they never really were all that tough to begin with. Maybe we've all just been fed a romanticized image of the western folk hero."

Her worst fears confirmed, Sophy quickly lifted the bedside receiver. "Max, wait. Mother? This is Sophy. That's Max on the other extension. He, uh, came by early this morning. I'm taking him to see some of the local sights." Frantically Sophy rushed into the conversation, desperate to correct the impression her mother must have gotten when Max answered her daughter's phone so early in the morning.

"I see," Anna Bennet began, only to be interrupted by Max again.

"Sophy's been very gracious to me, Dr. Bennet," he drawled easily. Where the hell had he picked up that faint Texas drawl? "She and I grilled steaks last night and this morning we're going to have breakfast together. Then we'll have to see about making some plans for the rest of the day."

"You're having breakfast together?" Anna Bennet

inquired with a mother's deep interest. "It's rather early for Sophy."

"You can say that again. She's still in bed. I was just about to take her some coffee, in fact, to help her get her eyes open," Max chuckled fondly.

"Max just arrived, mother," Sophy put in abruptly. "He caught me a bit unprepared." Shut up, Max, she begged silently. For God's sake, just shut up!

"How's your husband?" Max was saying cheerfully. "Good. Tell him I got a chance to read that paper he gave me on Jordan curves. Fascinating."

"He'll be looking forward to discussing it with you when you get back to Chapel Hill," Anna Bennet said. "And I'm so glad you and Sophy are hitting it off well. You know, Sophy was hanging around with some cowboy, last we heard, and her father and I were a trifle nervous about the relationship, to say the least."

"Mother!"

"No need to worry about the cowboy," Max assured Dr. Bennet a little too smoothly. "He's not in the picture any longer. Rode his horse off into the sunset."

"Max!"

"Well, that's reassuring," Dr. Bennet said happily. "Sophy, dear, you know how I felt about that cowboy. When you lived in California I used to dread your getting involved with some long-haired surfer type. Then when you moved to Texas I had to worry about cowboys. Such a relief to know you're seeing a nice young man like Max. Why don't you talk Max into coming back to Chapel Hill with you next weekend?"

"Excellent idea," Max put in swiftly before Sophy could hedge.

"I'm sure he's much too busy . . ." Sophy tried valiantly.

"I can manage the time."

Sophy could practically see her mother's beaming

smile. "Fine. What time does the flight arrive at the Raleigh-Durham airport, Sophy dear? Your father and I will meet the plane."

"The flight gets in at ten-thirty," Sophy sighed, knowing she was beaten.

"Wonderful. We'll be there. Can't wait to see both of you. Oh, and Max, thank you so much for looking Sophy up down there in Dallas."

"Believe me," Max drawled, "it's been my pleasure. You don't have to worry about Sophy anymore, Dr. Bennet. I'll be looking after her here in Dallas."

"Well, of course, Max," Dr. Bennet said, sounding vaguely surprised he should even bother to mention the subject. "Paul and I both know you're a gentleman as well as an outstanding scholar. See you next weekend!"

"With pleasure," Max laughed. "I could use a couple of days back in an academic environment. You know what a thrill it is to get out into the real world and lend industry a hand," he added derisively. "Actually, the only thing that has made this trip worthwhile is Sophy."

"Goodbye, mother!" Sophy tried to infuse a certain amount of command into her voice, and fortunately the other two seemed to sense it.

"Goodbye, Sophy, dear. And goodbye to you, Max. See you soon."

Max and Sophy put down their separate extensions simultaneously, but Sophy's came down a good deal harder. "Damn it! Max, how could you!" she shouted.

He appeared in the doorway of her bedroom, coffee in hand, a charmingly bland expression of inquiry on his face. "How could I what?"

Hastily Sophy yanked the sheet up to her throat, blushing at the possessive gleam in his eyes as he surveyed her in bed. "What on earth were you thinking of, answering the phone at this hour? Do you have any notion at all of what my mother must be thinking? She'll be weaving all sorts of marriage plans around the two of us, if I know her. She's probably already planning on enrolling him at Harvard!"

"Enrolling who?" Max looked at her blankly.

"Their grandchild!"

"Oh, him. I was thinking of Princeton, myself. That's where I went to school. Best math department in the country . . ." He broke off to dodge the pillow Sophy hurled at him and managed the feat without spilling the coffee.

For some reason the casual masculine grace of the movement stirred memories of his lovemaking during the night, and Sophy grabbed another pillow in blind self-defense.

"Sophy, honey, wait a minute." Max grinned, coming forward with the coffee in a gesture of appeasement. "Just listen to me."

She ignored him but dropped the pillow back on the bed as she got to her feet and grabbed for her robe. "No, you listen to me, Dr. Travers. You can play all the male games you want and my parents can dream all the dreams they want, but I am not going to be the ball you big cats bat around for fun, is that clear? I'm going to live my own life. I will not be your mistress, in spite of what happened last night. I will not settle down to producing little wizards for my parents to educate. I am going to open my own business here in Dallas and I'm going to date all the cowboys I want to date. And if and when I ever decide to marry, I'll send you all an invitation."

"Sophy!" As Max set down the coffee cup, his voice lost its teasing tone. Suddenly it held ice and steel. "To begin with, I don't recall mentioning marriage."

"Then you shouldn't have answered that telephone and implied to my mother that we're sleeping together!" she stormed, inexplicably hurt by the way he brushed off the word *marriage*. What was the matter with her, anyway? Of course she had no intention of marrying him. Why should she want him to be thinking of it?

"But now that the subject of marriage has arisen," Max put in deliberately, "I think it should be discussed."

That made her even angrier. "It sounds like much too academic a subject for me. I'm going to take a shower!" She whirled. How dare he treat it so deliberately and . . . and *academically?*

"Now hold on just one damn minute, Sophy Bennet." Max reached for her and yanked her around to face him. His gray eyes glittered with sudden male dominance. It occurred to Sophy that Max had undergone a dangerous transformation in the few days she had known him. That first night, when he had taken her out to dinner, he had been far more diffident and unassertive. She would never have guessed that in such a short time she would find herself not only seduced by him but intimidated on something other than an intellectual level.

"Let me go, Dr. Travers!"

"In a moment, Miss Bennet. There are a few things we should get settled first. What happened last night doesn't just get wiped out by a phone call from your mother, or because you're having second thoughts this morning. You're mine now. I told you that last night, and what's more important, you admitted it."

"I was . . . was caught up in an emotional, highly charged situation and I . . . I . . ."

"Are you going to claim I took advantage of you again? That you were emotionally vulnerable and I pushed you into bed? Don't bother, Sophy. It won't wash. You and I are definitely, undeniably *involved,* whether you like it or not. We're having an affair—"

"Two nights in bed together doesn't constitute an affair!"

"It does in our case," he retorted coldly. "Furthermore, I have some surprisingly primitive feelings on the subject of fidelity. Don't threaten me with cowboys ever again, because if I ever catch you with another cowboy or any other man, I'll beat you so thoroughly you'll think studying differential calculus was a treat by comparison!"

Sophy couldn't believe her ears. "And to think I once considered possessiveness in a man rather quaintly attractive, a sign of affection. But it's nothing but the basic male ego at work, isn't it? You think that because you've made love to me a couple of times you can set down all kinds of rules!"

"I haven't just made love to you a couple of times, Sophy Bennet," he gritted. "I have also fought another man for you and I have had you surrender completely in my arms. That gives me all kinds of rights, and I'm sorry if you don't like the possessiveness. It's a little new to me, too. I haven't ever felt quite this way about a woman before. But I'm damn well not going to go back to the stage where you walk all over me."

"I never tried to walk all over you! I simply tried to put as much distance as possible between us!" she cried wretchedly.

"Well, we're not going back to that stage either," he vowed, hauling her against his half-nude body. "I've worked too hard to get close to you!" He crushed her mouth under his, ignoring Sophy's impotent attempts at freeing herself.

She was terribly vulnerable, trying to battle him while she stood nearly naked in his arms, Sophy realized hysterically. All the memories of last night's passion were still too strong, especially in these surroundings—the rumpled bed; the memory of the way his shoulders had blocked out the moonlight when he'd lowered himself to her in the middle of the night. Even the scent of their lovemaking seemed to hover in the air. And they all contrived to leave her without any weapons when he forced his kiss on her lips.

God help her, Sophy thought agonizingly as she felt her body's reaction to Max's embrace, she was falling in love with the man. This wasn't mere sexual attraction, and it wasn't anything like what she had known with Nick Savage. She would be fooling herself terribly if she pretended she wasn't falling in love with Max Travers. And it was all so hopeless. He was so very wrong for her. Just as wrong as she would be for him. She would not be his crayons!

"Sophy," Max groaned huskily, "don't be afraid of me or of what we have together."

She shivered in his grasp, but whatever she would have said was lost in his deep kiss. When he lifted his head, they both knew the fight had gone out of her. Wordlessly she freed herself and headed for the shower.

Over breakfast forty minutes later she tried the rational approach. Pouring herself another cup of coffee, she took a deep breath and plunged in. "Max, have you given any real thought at all to what everyone's going to think if you go back to Chapel Hill with me next weekend?"

"Sure. They'll think we're passionately in love." His smile was very bland and very dangerous.

She must never forget for one moment that the intelligence behind those smoky eyes was formidable, Sophy reminded herself. Men like this had always been intimidating, but since she had left the academic world behind they had never posed a real threat to her. Now this man had moved into a sphere in which she should have been more than able to hold her own. And he was outmaneuvering her. He was ably assisted by her own traitorous emotions.

She had to fight or go under the tidal wave that threatened to engulf her.

"Well, we'll just have to make very sure that folks back in North Carolina don't accidentally get the wrong impression, won't we?'' she said with a smile every bit as bland as his own. But she could still hear the satisfaction in her mother's voice.

And I'll have to make damn sure I learn how to stay out of Max Travers's bed, she added with grim conviction.

8

On Monday morning Sophy walked into the offices of S & J Technology with a briefcase full of business-oriented magazines lifted off her coffee table and a profound thankfulness that Max had displayed a certain forbearance the night before. He had allowed himself to be sent home after dinner, much to Sophy's astonishment.

She hadn't questioned her luck, but she did question the emptiness of her apartment after he'd gone. Briskly she thrust aside the thought and walked toward Marcie's desk with firm purpose.

The blond looked up expectantly, a bit surprised.

"Marcie, we need to talk."

Warily Marcie bit her lip. "I know. It was a stupid idea, wasn't it? Of course you don't want to go through with it. And now that I've had the weekend to think it over, I don't either." She sighed. "I want to make it to the top, and I'm willing to be a little ruthless to get there, but I guess the truth is I'm not willing to compromise myself."

Sophy smiled. "I had a hunch you'd feel this way. But there's something else we need to talk about. Let's go down to the cafeteria and get some coffee."

"But it's too early to take a break," Marcie noted uneasily.

"Believe me, taking an early break is the last thing we should spend time worrying about. Marcie, this is important."

"All right."

Fifteen minutes later they secluded themselves at a corner table with two cups of hot coffee. A few members of junior management cast displeased glances at the pair of secretaries who had dared to take an unofficial break, but nothing was said.

"I don't know what got into me on Thursday," Marcie began unhappily. "I was so damned furious over being rejected for that promotion. I let my temper get the better of me."

"And I was just as angry over the fool I made of myself with Max Travers." Sophy couldn't bring herself to explain about the manner in which she'd run to Max to warn him and how everything had blown up in her face. There was no point, she told herself. This was a time for action. "Both of us let our anger get the best of us for a while. But when all is said and done, we really were rather justified, don't you think?"

Marcie smiled wryly. "Oh, yes. I think we both had justification."

"When dealing with a large corporation, a certain amount of subtlety is necessary," Sophy murmured thoughtfully as she stirred cream into her coffee. "And that applies to the fine art of teaching a lesson."

Marcie stared at her. "What are you talking about, Sophy?"

135

"I think the management of S & J needs a lesson."

"What kind of lesson."

"It needs to learn that mere secretaries should be taken a bit more seriously in the future."

"Sophy, you look very dangerous right at this moment," Marcie observed.

"I'm feeling a little dangerous. And a little reckless. We're going to find you a job, Marcie."

"A job!"

"Ummm. Oh, not here at S & J. We're just going to make sure that S & J appreciates what it lost when it loses you."

Marcie grinned. "A pleasant thought, but I don't see how we can manage that."

Sophy opened her briefcase and drew out a handful of booklets. Automatically Marcie leaned over to read the titles. "*Women in Business? Successful Women? Profiles of Successful Women and their Corporations?* Sophy, what are you going to do?"

"Find you a job at management level in one of the female-run technology firms profiled in these pamphlets. Oh, there aren't a lot of them because most such firms are run by men. But there are a couple, and all we need is one good one." She fanned out the pamphlets and grinned. "Pick a company, Marcie. Any company."

"And then what?"

"Then we convince that company they can't survive without you," Sophy said simply.

"What if the company doesn't happen to have any job openings?"

"It will. A good company always has openings for brilliant managers."

"And how are we going to make me look brilliant? The only jobs I have on my résumé are secretarial positions!"

"We start by rewriting your résumé," Sophy said. "And we go from there."

"Sophy, I get the feeling I'm seeing a new side of you."

"Not really. I just haven't had much chance to display this side before now," Sophy laughed.

Throughout the rest of the day, Marcie snatched every spare moment to study the magazines and pamphlets Sophy had given her. While she did so, Sophy concealed a copy of her friend's résumé among the pile of papers on her desk and surreptitiously made notes.

"It's too bad no one realizes just how much a good secretary really learns in the process of her work," Sophy noted at one point.

"I'm tired of waiting for recognition. You know the first thing I'm going to do when I get a high-level position, Sophy? Hire a male secretary."

"One with good legs?"

"Go ahead and laugh. I'm going to do it. It will be a symbolic action."

"I'd rather like to see Max Travers working as someone's secretary," Sophy decided wistfully. "The man can't even type."

As if the thought of him had conjured him up, the phone on Sophy's desk rang. Before she even said hello, she had an instinctive knowledge of who would be on the other end of the line.

"Sophy? I'm going to have to stay late with the programmer and work on this processing model this evening. I was planning to take you out to dinner tonight, but it looks like we'll have to postpone it. I'll call you later this evening."

Sophy heard the preoccupied note in his voice and almost found it endearing. The wizard at work. It was amazing, actually, that he'd even remembered to call. She knew a sense of relief mixed with a very real disappointment at the information that she would be spending the evening alone. "That will be fine, Max."

Her sense of disappointment had become anxiety by

that evening, when she analyzed the situation. She was aware of feeling pressured, trapped and terrified at the prospect of being in love with a man who was totally wrong for her.

How could Dr. Maximilian Travers ever really love and respect a woman who wasn't his intellectual equal? And how could she love a man who was destined to spend his life in an ivory tower?

"What I want is a man who can laugh with me as well as make love to me," she muttered aloud as she lay stretched out under the kitchen sink, preparing to fix the leaking fitting. "I want a man who lives life down here on my ordinary, humdrum level, not in the rarefied atmosphere of an academic tower. Damn sink. I want a man who can respect my abilities. A man who really thinks I'm his equal, not a toy he can play with. I'm not a pack of crayons, for crying out loud!"

The doorbell cut into the monologue.

"Oh, for pity's sake!" she exclaimed, as a box of soap nearby fell over when she scrambled out from under the sink. Sophy glared at it and at the evidence of the leak she had set out to fix. Then, grumbling, she headed for the door. Max Travers was on the threshold.

"What I really want," she gritted, waving the wrench at him, "is a man who knows how to fix a sink, unclog a toilet and grill a steak!"

Max's gaze went from the menacing wrench to the yellow tee shirt and orange trousers Sophy was wearing. Then his eyes went to the smudge on her nose and he smiled. "You want a plumber who can cook?"

"This is not funny!" She glared at him and then thrust the wrench into his hand. "Here. Show me you can do something useful in the world. We don't need more people who can think in five dimensions at the same time; we need people who can fix leaky plumbing. Cheap. What good is a man who can't fix a faucet?"

His eyes slitted as he looked down at the wrench. "You're in a swell mood, aren't you?"

"I mean it, Max. If you can't fix my faucet, just get in your car and go back to your hotel!"

"Sophy, I came here tonight to talk to you, not to fix your sink," he began reasonably, stepping inside the door and shutting it firmly behind him.

"Well, I don't have time to talk."

"Listen, honey, why don't you just call a plumber? Or the apartment manager?"

"At this hour of the night? It's nearly ten o'clock," she exploded. "One doesn't call managers or plumbers at ten o'clock at night unless it's a real emergency!"

He frowned. "Well, isn't it?"

"Max, all that is necessary is to use this wrench to tighten up a loose fitting on the pipe under the sink," Sophy retorted with exaggerated patience. She spun around on her heel and stalked back to the kitchen. "I realize that someone with a Ph.D. in mathematics might find such simple household repairs beyond his ability, but the rest of us have learned to take care of the little problems in life."

"Sophy . . ."

She heard the incipient irritation in his voice and ignored it. "Go away, Max. Tonight I need a man who knows and understands the real world, not a mathematician."

"Damn it, Sophy, give me the wrench!" He yanked it out of her hand just as she was about to lower herself back under the sink.

Sophy looked at him in astonishment. He was scowling rather fiercely. "Forget it, Max. I don't want a bigger leak than the one I've already got."

"I'll fix your damned sink!"

"You don't know how to fix a sink!"

"I learned how to grill a steak, didn't I? You said

yourself there are some things men are supposed to know instinctively. Well, I'm a man and I've got instincts like every other man. I'll put my instincts up against those of any dumb cowboy you can find in Texas! Now, get out of my way, woman. I'm going to fix the plumbing."

Sophy blinked and found herself stepping aside. She thought about telling him he'd cooked a lousy steak, but for some reason she couldn't do it. He looked so determined to fix the sink that she didn't have the courage to refuse him the opportunity. He was already examining the unique shape of the wrench in his hand. The next thing she knew he was crouching under the sink, eyeing the shape of the fittings. She watched him check the position of the leak, and then his hand tentatively went to the fitting above it.

"That's the one," she grudgingly admitted, kneeling beside him and peering at the piping.

"Geometry," he muttered. "Simple geometry."

"You fix plumbing your way and I'll fix it mine. I don't use geometry!"

He leaned down and turned over on his back, sliding under the curved pipe. "This," he said in satisfaction, "is going to be a snap compared to grilling a steak."

Sophy got to her feet with a muffled groan. What was she going to do if he succeeded in actually fixing the damn fitting? "As long as you're down there . . ." she began.

"If you're going to make me spend the whole evening working on your plumbing, you can darn well think again. One fitting is all I'm going to do tonight."

"What I was going to say," she shot back far too sweetly, "is that as long as you're down there, I thought I could give you some advice."

"Wonderful."

"Don't waste any more time working up a fake

computer math model of that processing system. I can tell you right now that Marcie isn't going to steal it."

He paused and she wondered at the sudden stillness in him. "You're sure?"

"I'm sure."

Another pause. "What about, uh, Younger's big charade?" he finally asked carefully. "Our posing as lovers and all."

"Oh, that can stand as it is," Sophy said airily.

Another pause. Longer this time. "Mind telling me why?"

"I've got plans of my own. Besides, we'll never be able to convince Younger that his scheme won't work. For the time being I want to act as though I'm still following orders."

"Sophy . . ." He sounded abruptly worried.

"Don't fret, Max. I'll explain everything when it's all over. I'm just telling you a bit now so you won't waste your time dummying up a fake printout. You can let Younger think you're still working on it, though."

"Sophy, I don't know what you're up to, but I don't like it."

"Don't worry about it, Max. This is my world. I know what I'm doing."

"I do not want you getting into any trouble," he began adamantly.

"The only trouble I have at the moment is a leaking faucet. How are you doing down there?"

"I don't know yet."

"There was one other thing I wanted to mention."

"I knew it," he groaned. "What is it?"

Sophy took hold of all the fortitude she possessed. "Max, I am not going to sleep with you again. Is that very, very clear?"

There was a sudden loud clang as something metallic scraped harshly along something else that was also metallic and then fell on the floor of the cupboard.

"Max! Are you all right?"

"Damn it to hell," Max growled.

"What's wrong?" she asked anxiously, going down on her knees to glance inside the cupboard.

"Nothing." The single word came out sounding like a curse. It was followed by another four-letter word that was definitely of the "expletive deleted" variety. "I'm just fixing the darned sink."

Sophy climbed back to her feet, frowning worriedly. "Oh. Well, did you hear what I said, Max?" Somehow it was easier having this very necessary conversation with him trapped under the sink. Sophy realized that the last thing she wanted to do was to have to look him in the eye while she told him she wouldn't go to bed with him.

"I heard you. Would you please hand me a rag?" One strong arm extended itself from the confines of the cupboard. Wordlessly Sophy stuffed a rag into the waiting fingers. "Thank you," Max said very politely, and went back to work. Several moments passed. Sophy began to grow restless.

"Max?"

"Hmmm?"

She cleared her throat. "Max, I mean it. I know I haven't given you any reason to think I have willpower, but I assure you—"

"What I'd really like at the moment, Sophy, is a drink. I think the fitting is going to stay tight now." He began to inch his way out of the cupboard. Then he was crouching in front, surveying his handiwork while he wiped his hands on the rag. He looked rather pleased with himself, Sophy thought, and squelched an inner groan of dismay. "You know," he announced, "that wasn't really too hard. It's just a matter of analyzing the situation and then applying the wrench in the proper manner. Take a look."

Sophy slanted him a long glance and then obediently bent down to check his workmanship. "It looks like it's stopped leaking," she agreed cautiously, and realized almost at once that wasn't enough. He was hovering beside her like a proud artist showing off his master-piece. Max wanted some genuine applause, and for some damn fool reason she couldn't resist giving his ego the stroking it wanted. "You did a terrific job." She could have kicked herself for saying the words he wanted to hear. "It's definitely stopped leaking." What else could one say about a fixed pipe? She leaned into the cabinet and tested the once-loose fitting. "Oh, that's on a lot more securely than I could have managed," she added brightly. Idiot. What was the matter with her? But Sophy couldn't bring herself to denigrate his first attempt at fixing plumbing. "You're very useful around the house, Max. I really appreciate your help tonight. That leak has been pestering me for days."

"No problem," he declared smoothly, getting to his feet. "Now, about that drink?"

"Actually," she said carefully, "I was going to pop some popcorn and watch an old movie on television this evening." Best to scare him out of the house before things got dangerous, Sophy told herself firmly. And she *had* been planning to watch the film.

He looked closely at her. "What old movie?"

"Nothing you'd be interested in, I'm sure," she said quickly. "It's one of those old science-fiction thrillers from the early fifties. You know, *The Eggplant That Ate Seattle* or something. You wouldn't like it at all."

"Why are you going to watch it?" he asked, leaning back against the counter.

"Because those old science-fiction flicks are hilari-ous," she said without thinking.

"I could use a good laugh after working on that damn program all evening and coming home to fix broken plumbing." Max rubbed the back of his neck in a gesture of weariness.

Sophy flinched at his use of the word "home" and

narrowed her eyes. "It will keep you up rather late, Max. If you're tired, you should go back to the hotel and get some rest."

"I can rest sitting on your couch watching the film. Where's the popcorn? I haven't had popcorn in ages." He glanced around the kitchen in anticipation.

"Max . . ."

"There's the corn popper. Up on top of your refrigerator. I'll get it down for you." He reached up to lift the machine down before she could find any words of protest. "Now, where's the oil?"

She grimaced. "It *has* been a long time since you had popcorn, hasn't it? That's one of the new air poppers. It doesn't use oil."

"Oh, yeah?" He glanced down at the machine in his hands. "How does it work?"

"You mean the physics of it?" she drawled, rummaging around in the small pantry for the popcorn. "I wouldn't have the vaguest idea. All I know is that you dump the corn in here and turn the sucker on. Presto! Popcorn."

"Fascinating."

"Uh-huh. Something tells me you're not going to be equally fascinated by this movie, Max," Sophy warned above the roar of the popping machine. "Are you sure you shouldn't be heading back to the hotel? You must be tired."

He gave her a level glance. "I'll survive."

She sucked in her breath. "I meant it, you know. You can't spend the night here, Max." She studied the growing pile of fluffy popcorn in the bowl on the counter.

"Are you afraid of me, Sophy?" His voice was low and gentle.

"I've behaved like a fool with you. I suppose we're all a little afraid of people who can make fools out of us."

"Look at me, honey."

Her head lifted warily. There was a curiously earnest gleam in his smoky eyes. It made her even more uneasy. "Max, please, I . . ."

"Don't be afraid of me, Sophy. Just relax. Treat me like a man, not a mathematician," he said with a faint edge of humor curving his mouth. "Give me a chance, honey. I told you I've got all the normal instincts."

"I've already encountered your normal instincts!" she snapped, switching off the popper. "On at least two different occasions. And as far as I'm concerned, that's twice too often. I meant what I said, Max. There will be no more sex between us! Now, if you're going to stay and watch this movie and eat my popcorn, you'll have to give me your word of honor as a gentleman that you won't force yourself on me."

He sighed, folding his arms across his chest. "Sophy, listen to me."

"Your word, Max."

"All right, all right. My word as a gentleman and a scholar. You can eat your popcorn in peace."

She chewed her lip and then nodded, accepting his promise. "Okay. You can stay. But you won't like it."

"Not being able to make love to you? I know I won't like it, but I'll live."

"I meant the film! You won't like the film!" she corrected waspishly as she carried the popcorn out into the living room and set the bowl down on the coffee table. Then she switched on the television.

"How can you be so sure of what I'll like and not like?" he demanded, following her into the front room.

"Believe me, this is not going to be your kind of film. The science in it is shoddy in the extreme. Mostly, it's completely lacking. Lots of bug-eyed monsters and mad scientists."

"I know a few of those, myself," he retorted equably. "Monsters or mad scientists?"

"Mad scientists. Hey, the film's in black-and-white."

"I told you it was old. These were pretty low-budget flicks." She sat down beside him on the couch and reached for the popcorn. "Just let me know when you get bored and want to leave."

"I'll let you know," he promised sardonically.

But he didn't get bored. Much to Sophy's surprise, he joined with her in cheering for the monster and booing the newspaper reporter and the good scientist who were trying to stop him. The corny dialogue and ridiculously old-fashioned special effects sent Sophy off into gales of laughter, and Max was not far behind. Together they wolfed down the entire bowl of popcorn and gave the monster a lot of advice on how to survive. But at last the creature went down, drawn under the sea in a whirlpool created by the scientist.

"Gone but not forgotten," Sophy pronounced. "He'll return, mark my words. You can't keep a good monster down."

"I hope not. I'd like to see him return. He was a fairly decent sort of monster. Not his fault the humans kept getting in his way. All he wanted was to feed off the energy in those bombs." Max leaned his head back against the couch, his legs stretched out in front of him. He glanced at Sophy. "Thanks."

"For what? The popcorn?" she asked lightly.

"And the film. I've never seen anything quite like it."

"Obviously you had a deprived childhood." She smiled. "Personally, I would have had a deprived one, too, if I hadn't snuck downstairs late at night to watch television. I also nourished myself during my formative years with a pile of super-hero comics I kept stashed under my mattress. I read them with a flashlight under the covers."

"I didn't get to read a comic until I was in college," Max said quietly. "Not even the funny pages from the newspaper. My parents thought they were silly and frivolous. To tell you the truth, I agreed with them."

"They are silly and frivolous. That's why they're good for you."

Max smiled. "You're good for me," he said softly, reaching out to gather her into his arms.

Instantly Sophy was on her feet, scooping up the empty bowl of popcorn. "I think it's time you went home, Max." Turning her back on him, she headed for the kitchen. Behind her she heard him slowly get to his feet.

"It's a long drive back downtown . . ."

"Then you should have left earlier."

"Before I found out whether the monster or the scientist won?" he protested, ambling into the kitchen behind her.

She swung around, her chin lifted proudly. "I meant what I said, Max. You're not staying the night." There was almost a pleading note in her words.

He looked down at her for a long moment, and she could read nothing in the depths of his eyes. Then he lifted his hand to toy with the curls that fell on her shoulders. "Such wonderful hair," he breathed, leaning forward to inhale the scent of it.

"Good night, Max," she whispered huskily. Already she could feel the flickering sensual tension beginning to flare between them. But this time she would not succumb.

"Sophy, at least let me kiss you," he murmured in that low, persuasive voice that he always seemed to use when he got close to her. It played havoc with her senses. Sophy's fingernails bit into the softness of her palm, but she held fast to her resolve.

"No, Max."

"I want you, sweetheart."

"No, Max."

He groaned and abruptly hauled her into his arms, the flash of desire in his eyes burning strongly for a moment. "You can keep me out of your bed tonight, but you owe me this kiss, damn it!"

"Why?" she challenged, bringing up her hands to push against his chest.

"Because I fixed your leaky plumbing!" Then he was drinking his fill from her lips as if he anticipated dying of thirst in the near future. His mouth moved on hers with the sensual, plundering provocation she had already learned was her nemesis. But before she could summon the will to resist, he freed her, stepping away with an annoyed, frustrated and dangerously male expression on his hard features. "If you'll excuse me, I'll get my coat and be on my way," he drawled far too politely.

Sophy waited restlessly in the kitchen for him to collect the old tweed jacket from the hall closet. She heard the closet door open and close, and then she heard nothing more. There was no sound of his footsteps coming back down the hall. Damn that man! If he thought he could get away with forcing his way into her bedroom, he had a few things to learn about her!

"Max?" she called menacingly as she went down the hall. There was no answer. "Max, where are you?" The light was off in the bedroom. If that man was playing games with her, she would be furious!

"I'm in here, Sophy," his answer finally came, sounding distant and vague, as if he were only half-aware of her call. The sound of his voice was emanating from her sewing room.

"Max? What in the world are you doing in here?" she demanded, pushing open the door.

"Just looking." He was bent over the large worktable, examining the pattern pieces lying on top of a length of material. He seemed as intent and curious as if he were looking at an oversized math problem. "How does all this work, Sophy?" he asked, glancing up briefly as she came into the room. "These lines on the pattern—they're very precise."

"Well, of course they're precise. Start out with a sloppy pattern and you'd wind up with a sloppy garment," she muttered, moving to stand on the opposite side of the table.

"The angles here—"

"Those are called darts. You use them to create shape in a piece of flat fabric, to help shape material to the human body. People have a lot of odd curves and angles on them, you know." A touch of humor laced her voice. "The wider the angle of the dart—"

"The greater the curving shape that will be created." He nodded at once, looking very serious.

"Well, yes," she agreed, momentarily surprised.

"What are these parallel lines for?"

"Pleats. They give fullness where I want it but with a sense of control."

He traced another line with the tip of his finger. "And this?"

"Just a seam line."

"And this curved section?"

"A collar. I want it to roll a bit, so I'm adding extra width at the outside edge." She leaned across the table to show the point where she had adjusted the outer curve of the pattern piece. "The more the neckline curve flattens, the greater the roll I'll get in the finished collar."

Max nodded again, looking surprisingly intrigued. Then he walked across the room and stood before a large sketch of a deceptively simple dress. "I think I can visualize how you get from the pattern to the finished garment," he said after a moment. "But there's no way on earth I could do it. And I can't even begin to figure out how you get from the sketch to the basic pattern. The original design is art. The pattern is a mathematical procedure. The final construction is art again. Amazing."

Sophy stood staring at him, equally amazed. No one

from Max's world, not even her parents, had ever shown any interest in her work. The designing and construction of a garment were loosely labeled "sewing" and relegated to a pile of topics deemed mundane or frivolous. For a moment Sophy experienced a bond of communication, an understanding, that she rarely knew when dealing with someone from Max's world. He understood enough of her work to appreciate it. Her heart warmed.

She was still staring when Max turned around, swung his coat over his shoulder and walked back across the room to brush her mouth gently with his. "I'll go now, Sophy. But there's one other thing . . ."

"Yes, Max?" What was she hoping for? That he might insist on staying?

"I think you should call off whatever little scheme you've got going with Marcie Fremont. The woman suggested corporate espionage to you once. No telling what she might involve you in now."

The warmth that had crept into her began to fade. "I know what I'm doing, Max. And the scheme isn't Marcie's idea. It's all mine."

He frowned. "Sophy . . ."

"Don't worry. This won't affect you. All I'm going to do is find Marcie another job," she said too easily.

"Sophy, I . . ." He broke off on a sigh of resignation. "You're not going to tell me what's going on, are you?"

"Last time I did that, you ran straight to Graham Younger."

He winced. "I thought it was for the best."

"And look what you got us involved in."

"I can see this conversation is going nowhere. Good night, Sophy. I'll see you at work."

And then he was gone, leaving her with a new uncertainty and a new sense of ambivalence to add to her already unmanageable list of problems concerning Dr. Max Travers.

9

The following morning Sophy put the next step of her plan into action. Marcie had selected her ideal company, a California firm run by a woman. It was a high-technology company competing in many of the same areas as S & J.

"I could really make a contribution there," Marcie said earnestly over coffee. "And there seems to be a fairly equal spread of men and women in management. It's an aggressive young firm, but it seems well founded financially. From what I can tell, though, the staff seems to be pretty heavy on technological skills and rather light on business experience. Maybe they could use someone like me who has a slightly different background."

"If that's the one you want, that's the one we'll go for," Sophy said firmly. "Oh, by the way, here's your new résumé." She handed the paper to Marcie.

"But, Sophy, this doesn't even sound like me," Marcie gasped after a moment's close concentration.

"This makes me sound . . . well, fabulous. Like I've been practically running S & J since I got here!"

"What we're going to do next," Sophy announced smugly, "is get some letters from S & J management testifying to that."

"What?" Marcie looked startled.

"Let's go back to work, Marcie. I have some letters to write."

The letters eulogizing the contributions of one Marcie Fremont to S & J Technology went out to be signed by appropriate members of management that afternoon. Sophy judged it wise not to allow Marcie to see them before they went out. The blond was liable to be somewhat appalled by the liberties Sophy had taken.

"Actually, it's just a bit of creative writing," Sophy had explained when Marcie anxiously tried to read one. "Now go back to work. You've got your hands full doing my tasks as well as your own today."

The first letter was slipped into a pile of correspondence waiting to be signed by the vice-president in charge of planning. It graphically detailed Marcie's expertise in that area. The second letter went into a stack sitting on the desk of the president's assistant. In each case Sophy waited until the executive's personal secretary was out of the office. Then she waylaid the secretaries and chatted with them while their bosses signed the letters while hurriedly pausing by the secretaries' desks. It was an easy matter to remove the letters from the piles of legitimate correspondence when the secretaries turned their backs.

A few more such letters from important people in the company joined the first two. And then Sophy wrote the cover letter that was to accompany Marcie's résumé and letters of recommendation. This she let Marcie see.

"But, Sophy, it says here I'm sending this packet of information at the request of their manager in charge of executive recruiting! I didn't get any such request."

"Details."

"Sophy, you're sending the letter to the vice-president instead of Personnel."

"The first rule in dealing with a corporation is to ignore Personnel," Sophy assured her blithely, stuffing the packet into a large envelope. "No one ever got a really high-level position by going through Personnel."

Marcie stared at her in wondering admiration. "You seem to know your way around corporations."

Sophy grinned. "I should. I've been studying them very carefully for several years. When I start my own business, I want to know as much as possible. Believe me, the vice-president who receives this packet will never figure out that his recruiting officer knows nothing about it."

"I'm fascinated. What's next?"

"A phone call later on in the week after we know this envelope has had a chance to reach its destination."

"Phone call? From whom?"

"From Graham Younger's office, of course, complaining loudly that the other firm is attempting to pirate you away. A few threats and requests to please not tempt you. That sort of thing."

"From Younger's office?" Marcie gasped.

"That's what the other company will think."

"Who's really going to make the call, Sophy?" Marcie demanded with an arched brow.

"Me."

"Oh, my."

"Believe me, hype is everything. Once they learn that S & J is frantic not to let you go, nothing will keep that California company from hiring you."

"Sophy, something tells me I should stick around here a little longer and learn from you!"

Sophy laughed. "I won't be here much longer myself."

The phone call went as planned. By the time Sophy

hung up the receiver she was feeling very pleased with herself. Now it was all a matter of time.

"But something tells me they won't take long beating a path to your door, Wonder Woman," she told Marcie with a laughing smile.

Max was aware of an oddly possessive sense of pride as he escorted Sophy off the plane and into the waiting lounge of the Raleigh-Durham airport. She was as vivid and colorful as ever today, he thought. Her expressive face was full of anticipation and pleasure at the prospect of seeing her parents. Even without the added effect of the racy turquoise jumpsuit she was wearing and the tumble of thick curls cascading down to her shoulders, that face caught and held one's attention. It held his at any rate, he amended wryly. She certainly wasn't trying to hold him with sex!

He still had no clear idea of what she was up to with Marcie Fremont, but he had made a conscious decision not to question his luck. She was still playing out the charade demanded of her by Graham Younger and his associates. Right now that seemed to be all that mattered. He'd keep an eye on her and make sure she didn't get into any real trouble. In the meantime, he'd told Younger's assistant that the plan was going well. They had agreed to let him manage things by himself until the crucial juncture.

The fact that there wasn't going to be a "crucial juncture" didn't particularly worry him. All he cared about was keeping Sophy within reach.

Until this past week Dr. Max Travers hadn't realized that he could actually lie alone in bed and hunger physically for a particular woman. The knowledge left him unsettled and restless, but it didn't affect him as badly as knowing that what he felt was not just a craving of the body. He found himself making every excuse imaginable just to be around Sophy. The time that he wasted running back and forth to her office to check up on the various reports she typed for him was appalling!

"Mom! Dad!" Sophy was running ahead, leaving Max to bring her small under-the-seat bag. He had a momentary wish that the obviously feminine case weren't such an eye-catching shade of magneta. Then he grinned to himself. If a man was going to hang around Sophy Bennet very long, he would have to get used to being seen amid a lot of color.

Max watched a little wistfully as Sophy threw herself into her parents' arms. Then he took a firm grip on himself. One of these days, he vowed, Sophy would learn to greet him that enthusiastically.

"Sophy, dear, it's so good to see you again." Anna Bennet smiled warmly as she hugged her daughter. The older woman was something of a contrast to Sophy, and Max had to look closely to see the faint traces of resemblance. They were there in the curling hair that Anna Bennet kept severely trimmed, and in the gentle shape of the nose, but they weren't startlingly obvious. Dr. Bennet wore a conservatively cut tweed skirt, a sweater and a pair of sensible shoes.

Sophy's eyes, Max decided, came from her father, although his blue-green gaze seemed slightly faded compared to his daughter's vivid one. Paul Bennet was taller than his wife and daughter, his gray hair cut much like Max's. The realization made Max wince. Maybe he should think about getting his dark hair trimmed in a slightly less conservative style. Sophy might like it better. Paul Bennet was still a handsome man, his strong features revealing the intelligence and character that had shaped his career. He was dressed in a slightly rumpled tweed jacket, and in his shirt pocket there was a plastic pack of pencils and implements. The horn-rimmed glasses reminded Max uncomfortably of his own pair.

Watching Sophy flutter energetically among the three

of them as greetings were accomplished, Max realized just how different she was from himself and her parents. She was colorful and outrageous, whereas the other three were bland and conservative. She was lively and full of laughter while he and the Bennets were reserved and far quieter in their demeanor. Watching the Bennets interact with their daughter, Max had a flash of insight into just how difficult things must have been for Sophy at times. It had undoubtedly worked both ways, he decided. Paul and Anna Bennet must have had moments when they wondered whether or not their daughter had been a changeling, a mischievous elf substituted at birth for the quiet, serenely brilliant daughter who should have been theirs.

But there was love in the family, even if the three people concerned sometimes wondered how Paul and Anna Bennet had managed to produce such an unexpected sort of daughter. Max's sense of wistfulness grew. He had been everything his parents had wanted and more, and yet he'd never known this kind of family affection.

"Max! Glad you could make it," Paul Bennet said genially, extending his hand. There was genuine pleasure in the eyes that so resembled Sophy's, and Max relaxed. Sophy might not appreciate his interest in her, but her parents were quite content with him, he thought on a note of humor.

"Thank you, sir. To tell you the truth, I was glad of the excuse to take a break from Dallas." *And I'd have followed your daughter to the North Pole.*

"Miss North Carolina, do you?" Paul chuckled as he shepherded everyone to the baggage claim area.

Max cast an appreciative glance out at the rich green countryside. "Let's just say Dallas is a little different," he murmured dryly.

"Poor Max has been suffering greatly," Sophy informed everyone melodramatically. "Nearly three weeks of the real world and he's about to pine away."

"Sophy has done a great deal to cheer me up during the course of my exile," Max shot back smoothly, catching her eye and daring her to push the topic further. He received a speculative glance in return and then, much to his surprise, she moved on to another subject.

"What time is the ceremony and reception, Mom?" she asked brightly.

"Seven o'clock tonight. Did you bring something to wear?"

"What a silly question," Paul Bennet murmured as three huge magenta suitcases came trundling around the baggage belt.

Max grinned at the older man. "Sophy claims she likes to travel prepared."

Paul shook his head in wry affection. "She always did have a thing about clothes."

"I'll have you know that at least one of those suitcases is full of presents," Sophy tossed out indignantly as the two men picked up the colorful baggage. "After all, one can't go visiting an award-winning physicist without a few gifts!"

Max slid her a sidelong glance as he picked up the two heaviest cases and led the way out to the parking lot. She really was quite proud of her mother, he thought, in spite of her comments about academicians.

"Sophy's presents are always interesting, to say the least," Anna Bennet said with a knowing smile. She glanced at Max as the magenta cases were stowed in the back of the Bennets' car. "Has she had occasion to give you anything yet, Max?"

Max smiled as he slammed the trunk lid. "Yes, Sophy's given me some very special gifts," he said softly. He saw the sudden wariness in Sophy's eyes, and his smile broadened as he took her arm and guided her into the back seat of the car. "But I'm having a hard time finding out what she wants in return. Would you like me to drive, Dr. Bennet?"

"Thank you, Max." He handed over the keys. "It will give me a chance to talk to Sophy." He assisted his wife onto the seat alongside Sophy and then climbed into the front seat as Max started the car. "I understand the two of you have been seeing a lot of each other lately. Any surprises in the offing?"

There was a moment of electric silence during which Max considered a hundred different ways of saying he wanted Paul Bennet's daughter. But it was Sophy who rushed in to fill the breach.

"How did you know?" she demanded cheerfully. Max glanced quickly into the rearview mirror and caught the look of determination on her face. One thing was certain, she wasn't going to announce any engagement. "I've decided to open my own design boutique down in Dallas. I'm really very excited about it, aren't I, Max? Of course, I'll have to take out a loan, but I think I can get that. I made a dress for the woman who manages the loan department of my bank, and I'm sure she'll back me now that she's seen my work."

Another tense silence followed the exuberant announcement. It was Anna Bennet who broke it this time. "Oh, Sophy, dear, are you sure that's what you want to do? Have you given any more thought to going back for your master's degree? You know your father and I would love to have you get at least one more degree and we'd be more than happy to finance your educational costs."

Sophy took a deep breath. "Mom, I don't care if I never set foot on a campus again. Wasting time getting another degree is just about the last thing in the world I want to do. I'm going to open the boutique."

Her father coughed meaningfully. "But what about

you and Max? I understood the two of you were hitting it off rather well. If the two of you decide to . . . that is, why would you want to open a little clothing shop if you're going to be getting—"

"Dad, I think this is an appropriate moment to say quite clearly that Max and I have absolutely no plans for marriage, do we, Max?" Sophy challenged him from the back seat.

Max heard the defiant taunting in her voice and simultaneously sensed the questioning glances he was getting from both of the Doctors Bennet. Trust Sophy to find a way of putting him on the spot. Maybe the Bennets should have spent more time applying their palms to Sophy's sweet backside rather than force-feeding her quadratic equations.

"Your daughter, sir," he said coolly to Paul Bennet, "seems to have a certain aversion to marrying anyone with a Ph.D. after his name."

"Oh, is that the problem?" Anna Bennet chuckled from the back seat, patting Sophy's hand affectionately. "I'm sure you'll overcome her prejudice, Max. She always claimed she'd never marry a professor, but we've told her time and time again that when the right man comes along, she'll change her mind."

"Well, since I haven't changed my mind," Sophy muttered forcefully, "we have to conclude that the right man hasn't yet come along."

There was a painful pause as everyone in the car absorbed the full implications of her words. There was no doubt but that her statement hovered on being an outright insult. Sophy, herself, bit her lip in sudden anxiety, wishing she'd kept her mouth shut. But, damn it, she wasn't going to be pushed into anything, regardless of what her parents wanted! Max had created this mess by answering the phone last Sunday morning. Let him figure a way out of it.

Guiding the car along the stretch of freeway leading

toward the town of Chapel Hill, Max could almost read her thoughts. She was feeling pressured again and she was going to fight the pressure, just as she had been doing for so many years.

"I get the feeling that Sophy would rather, er, live in sin than compromise her principles where professors are concerned," he drawled.

"I think it should be noted at this juncture," Sophy began dryly, "that I haven't been given a choice where Max is concerned."

Paul Bennet turned in the seat to stare quizzically at his daughter. "What are you talking about, Sophy? For heaven's sake, girl, make sense!"

"Okay, I'll lay it on the line," Sophy retorted with obvious relish. "Max has not asked me to marry him. Therefore, this whole discussion is absolutely pointless, isn't it, Max?"

He flicked another glance in the rearview mirror, and this time it was Anna Bennet's questioning gaze he found there. His hands tightened on the wheel.

"I have learned," Max said evenly, in response to the uncomfortable silence in the car, "that if one wants the best results from Sophy, one doesn't *ask* her anything. One tells her."

Suddenly Paul Bennet laughed out loud and a moment later his wife joined him. "I think you may have the right approach, Travers. She's an independent little thing, isn't she?"

"Probably gets it from her parents," Max said gently.

Anna Bennet smiled contentedly. "Oh, we tried to make a proper daughter out of her, Max. Don't think we didn't try. But Sophy always went off on her own tangents. She brought home stray kittens instead of straight A's on her report cards. She read Nancy Drew stories when she should have been reading her Boolean algebra, and she was forever playing with scraps of fabric when she should have been playing with physics.

Every time I turned around, the child had a crayon in her hand instead of a pencil and a calculator. When she was five, my entire kitchen was decorated with designs for doll clothes."

And your house was filled with color and the unexpected, Max added silently.

"Mind you," Paul Bennet inserted quickly, "she has the basic ability; it's just that her interests have never been, well, properly focused. That's why we keep hoping she'll go back to school."

"Dad, you don't have to sell me to Max," Sophy drawled from the back seat. "He knows perfectly well that I'm not a wizard. No point trying to fool him."

Paul shifted uncomfortably in the front seat, and suddenly Max found himself grinning conspiratorially at the older man. "Sassy, rebellious and undisciplined," Max said, "but I would say that the genes are undoubtedly quite sound. Couldn't be anything else coming from you and Anna."

"Max Travers!" Sophy nearly choked on her outrage, but everyone else was laughing and a moment later she succumbed to the humor of the situation. Max was getting a little too fast on his feet, she decided wryly. He was starting to hold his own in areas that had been exclusively hers, like taunting wizards.

By seven o'clock that evening equilibrium had been restored to the Bennet household. Max had walked from the Bennets' to his own home a few tree-shaded blocks away, saying he would return in time to walk with them to the campus where the ceremonies were being held.

"I'm going to see if I can dig out a new nerd pack for the occasion," he'd murmured to Sophy on the way out.

"Good idea," she retorted. "Why don't you fill it with crayons instead of pens and pencils? Might set a whole new style on campus." She smiled saucily as he gave her a strange glance.

When he returned at seven, wearing his best tweed jacket and his newest tie—which was still about an inch too narrow—Sophy and her parents were ready to go.

"You look very charming tonight, Anna," Max said politely, meaning it. She was dressed more fashionably than usual in a striking black and white suit that complemented her refined, academic air.

"Sophy made this for me." Anna smiled, gesturing at the skirt and jacket. "It was one of the presents in the suitcase."

Max looked at Sophy. "I've heard people say she's a genius with clothing design," he said softly. Sophy herself was wearing one of her typically flashy outfits, a tiny, pencil-slim suit with a nipped-in jacket trimmed with broad lapels. The suit was white, the lapels shocking pink. "What was your present, Dr. Bennet?" he asked, nodding at Paul.

"A smoking jacket." Paul Bennet chuckled. "Never had one before. Sophy says it will go nicely with the image. I'm supposed to sit in front of the fire and smoke my pipe in it. Really, my boy, I think it's time you started calling me Paul," he added firmly as he pulled his wife's coat out of the closet.

"Thank you," Max murmured politely, his eyes on Sophy. "Are we ready?"

"Not quite," Sophy said abruptly, turning away to head down the hall toward the bedrooms. Her impossibly high heels made tantalizing tapping sounds on the parquet floor, and Max watched her until she disappeared.

In the bedroom she used whenever she visited her parents, Sophy opened one of the magenta suitcases and removed the last gift. Up until now she had been of two minds about whether or not to give it, but for some reason the decision had been made. Clutching it firmly in her left hand, she went back into the paneled living room where Max and her parents waited.

"Here," she said brusquely. "This one's for you, Max."

Behind the lenses of his glasses Max's smoky eyes flared for an instant before he lowered his gaze to the long, narrow box in her hand. "For me?" He looked as if he didn't know what to do with it, and Sophy found herself remembering all the Christmases and birthdays when his parents had forgotten to give him presents or had given him "learning" toys.

"Don't worry," Sophy murmured, "it's not an educational toy."

He grinned suddenly, taking the box with an eagerness that left her nonplussed. Wasting no time on the outer wrapping, Max tore off the paper and the small strip of ribbon and yanked open the box.

"A tie!" He lifted the length of silk fabric out of the tissue paper. For a long moment he simply stared at it, and then he looked at Sophy. "You made this?"

"Ummm." She nodded, feeling a little uncertain about her decision to give it to him. It wasn't really Max's style at all. Then again, could anyone truthfully say that Max had a style? "If you don't like it, I can always palm it off on Dad, here." The words were defensive and she knew it. Was she afraid of his rejecting the gift? What nonsense. How could it matter one way or the other? But it did. It mattered terribly.

"Sophy, it's beautiful. I've never seen anything like it." Max was turning it over in his hand, examining the delicate handwork on the other side, noting the way it had been cut on the bias. The silk was not a loud pattern, rather an unusually refined and conservative one, considering Sophy's basic tastes. It looked rich and elegant.

"You can make me one like that any time," Paul Bennet said to his daughter.

Anna Bennet looked bemusedly at the new clothes and the tie, and then at her daughter. "You really do have a certain talent, don't you, darling?"

Paul Bennet nodded agreement. "I hadn't quite realized . . ." He broke off as he peered over Max's shoulder. "Going to wear it tonight, Max?"

"You bet I am!" Max was already tearing free the old-fashioned narrow tie he was wearing, tossing it carelessly on a nearby chair. Then, collar flipped up, he stood in front of the living room mirror and knotted the new tie with careful precision. When the task was done, he stepped back and eyed his reflection with obvious satisfaction. "Thank you, Sophy. Thank you very much."

Before she realized his intention, he strode the three paces that separated them and kissed her soundly. As she stood there, blinking in wide-eyed surprise over her own actions, Max took her arm and guided her out the door. "Shall we go?" he asked. "Dr. Anna Bennet's fans will be waiting."

Anna Bennet laughed gently, her pleased eyes on the way Max was holding her daughter's arm. With her own arm linked in that of her husband, she traded a knowing glance with her mate. Then the four of them walked through the brisk evening toward the university campus.

Sophy watched the award ceremony with deep pride. Anna Bennet's accomplishments in the field of physics were known by many in the academic world, and the honors she received that evening were well deserved. No one knew that better than Sophy, and no one could have been prouder, unless it was Anna's husband, who glowed with pride and happiness.

The reception that followed the short ceremony was crowded with friends and colleagues of the Bennets' and of Max's. In fact, most of the academic community had turned out for the event. Sophy felt as if she had been plunged back into the world she had fought so long to escape. If it hadn't been for the fact that it was her mother who was being honored, she told herself as she hovered near the small hors d'oeuvre table, she would leave immediately. She'd always dreaded academic receptions. Lousy food and pompous people.

"Are you Sophy Bennet?" A somewhat rumpled-looking young man with wire-rimmed glasses, a corduroy jacket and curling hair that badly needed a cut smiled tentatively from the other side of the table.

Sophy smiled back, labeling him instantly and accurately as a graduate student. "Yes, I am."

The young man nodded in quick relief and adjusted his tie—a tie that was too narrow. "I'm Hal Anderson. A student of your mother's. She suggested I might like to meet you." His eyes darted curiously over her outrageously stylish appearance.

"I'm pleased to know you, Hal," Sophy said easily, helping herself to a pile of little cucumber sandwiches. "Was there some special reason you wanted to meet me?"

He turned a dull red. "Oh, no, well . . . that is, I, er, saw you standing over here and I sort of wondered aloud who you were, and your mother heard me and said you were her daughter and why didn't I come over and say hello."

Sophy nearly choked on her bite of cucumber sandwich and then recovered nicely. An academic pickup! She seemed to be rather popular with the academic community these days. Still, this was a student of her mother's and he really was rather sweet. "I'm glad you came on over, Hal." The young man relaxed slightly and smiled faintly. "What area are you specializing in?"

That was all the opening Hal Anderson needed. He plunged into a rousing discussion of solid-state physics that enabled Sophy to smile encouragingly a lot and munch cucumber sandwiches to her heart's content.

"Don't let Hal bore you to death," another man warned, wandering over to join in the discussion. "I'm Dick Santini. I'm in the math department."

"Oh, I'm quite fascinated with Hal's area of expertise. I'm sure he's going to make some outstanding contributions to his field," Sophy said smoothly. "And what about you, Dr. Santini? What area of research are you engaged in?"

Santini was well into a discussion of his work in spherical trigonometry, and Hal Anderson was putting in several more comments on physics, when two or three other graduate students and faculty members wandered up to join the discussion. Sophy found herself surrounded by earnest academicians, each eager to tell her about his line of work.

Across the room she briefly caught Max's eye and saw that he was beginning to frown as the group around Sophy grew. Cheerfully she smiled back, silently assuring him that she was quite content, and then she went back to orchestrating the discussion.

They followed her lead readily enough, and somehow her pile of cucumber sandwiches grew rather than shrank as eager hands sought to make her comfortable. Somewhere along the line Sophy realized just how well she was doing juggling all the different academic disciplines. Where had she picked up this marvelous social skill? Heretofore at such receptions, she'd always wound up standing alone, unable to maintain any kind of conversation.

It came from juggling members of corporate management, she decided in a flash of perception. The thought made her smile broaden. Some skills were useful in both worlds.

"Excuse me, gentlemen." Max's deep voice cut through the lively discussion like a hot knife through Jell-O. Sophy glanced up at him and found that there was a certain amount of fire behind the smoke of his eyes. Max was looking a bit dangerous. "Sophy, I came to take you outside for a breath of fresh air," he began determinedly, moving to stand possessively close.

"Oh, I'm doing fine, Max. Dr. Mortenson here has been keeping my glass full of sherry and I don't feel the heat at all. We were just having the most interesting discussion on the applications of probability theory in various disciplines. Dr. Santini has done some fascinating work on the subject of—"

"I'm aware of Dr. Santini's work," Max drawled dryly.

Good grief, Sophy thought in astonishment, Max *was* starting to exhibit a certain southwestern accent. Strangely enough, although it had annoyed her faintly in Nick Savage, it seemed rather attractive in Max.

Dr. Santini was looking vaguely uncomfortable under Max's assessing glance and hastened to fill in the conversational lapse. "Miss Bennet is very interested in quite a variety of topics, Max."

"Is she?"

Sophy moved to intercept. "Oh, yes, Max! After all, occasionally one should check up on investments, don't you think?"

Everyone in the group, including Max, stared at her blankly. "Investments?" Dr. Mortenson asked.

"Well, of course," Sophy laughed gently. "You, all of you"—she waved a graceful hand to include the entire academic campus—"represent a considerable investment on the part of the business world. Sizable investments should occasionally be monitored."

"I'm not quite sure what you mean," Hal Anderson said carefully.

Sophy grinned. "Gentlemen, where do you think the money for research and education comes from? It comes from business. Funding universities and colleges represents a long-range investment in the future. The corporate world, the *working* world, has its faults, but you have to admit that it has the guts to put its money where its mouth is, even when it isn't always sure of what the final outcome will be. If there's one thing the business world believes in, it's the future."

There was a pause while the group digested that. Finally Hal Anderson chuckled. "Not the most flattering way of looking at the matter, but I suppose it contains a good deal of truth. I guess academic elitism sometimes sets in around a campus."

Sophy nodded wisely. "And corporate elitism sometimes sets in around a large company. People are people. But the reality is that the academic world and the business world are interdependent. We need the education and skills and research done on campuses to further practical development in the business world. And you need the continuing financial investment and support of the business world to continue your education and research. We all benefit in the end."

In her own way, perhaps, Sophy realized, she had been just as guilty of elitism as any academician. With that realization came another: She was no longer intimidated by the academic world.

"I just hope," Dr. Santini said wistfully, "that you'll continue to check up on your investments occasionally. A bit of interaction between the academic and business worlds is always useful . . ."

"Definitely," Hal Anderson declared. "Would you like some more cucumber sandwiches, Sophy?"

"Or some more sherry, Miss Bennet?" Dr. Mortenson asked anxiously.

Max made a firm bid for Sophy's arm, wrapping it protectively around his own. "I promised Anna Bennet I would rescue her daughter and return her to her parents," he said smoothly. "Come along, Sophy. You've done enough investment counseling for the evening."

Sophy slid him a sidelong glance as he coolly led her

away. Her lips curved with inner laughter. "I think you may have spent too much time in Texas, Max. I'm seeing glimpses of lean, mean cowboy in you lately. Complete with accent."

He arched one brow over the rim of his glasses and there was a faintly sardonic twist to his mouth. "A good academician is always willing to learn, honey. I intend to get as good at handling you as you've gotten at handling members of a university faculty."

Sophy thought about that. "I did all right tonight, didn't I?"

"Sophy, honey, I've never seen you when you didn't do all right. Sometimes you scare the hell out of me!"

"You sound serious!"

"Professors of mathematics are always serious," he informed her. "And I will seriously consider beating you if I find you doing too many impromptu lectures on the interdependence of the academic world and the business world in front of an all-male audience!"

"Yes, Max, I do believe you've been a little too long in Texas." But in her heart Sophy was thinking about serious professors of mathematics. Was it possible she could be more to Dr. Max Travers than a pack of crayons? Would a serious academician like Max waste time pursuing a mere pack of crayons?

Together with that question came a pleasant feeling of having held her own very comfortably in a world that had always been distinctly uncomfortable.

Perhaps, as she had just lectured several members of the university faculty and staff, the two worlds were intertwined. More than she had realized, herself.

10

Max found himself unable to take his eyes off Sophy's profile as she sat beside him, staring out the jet's window. In another hour they would be back in Dallas. Back to where they started? The time in Chapel Hill seemed like a kind of truce that could be shattered again at any moment now that they were on their way back to Texas. There were so many questions. What was she up to with Marcie? How much longer would she be willing to play out the charade of having an affair with him for Graham Younger's benefit? How much time did he have?

Does she need me at all? Max wondered. *The way I need her?* Damn it to hell. What did you do with a woman who melted in your arms in bed but who kept you at arm's length outside it?

"I haven't thanked you for defending my boutique plans to my parents," Sophy said quietly, interrupting his thoughts. "It was very gracious of you to tell them you thought the idea was a good one and that you believe I have real talent in business as well as design."

Max leaned his head back against his seat. "I meant it, Sophy. Every word. You do have real talents as a designer and a businesswoman. Even I can tell that." He fingered the tie she had made. He was wearing it again today. "I think your parents appreciate your abilities. They just don't understand the business world enough to see how you could ever make a career out of what they've always considered a hobby."

"The academic world is their whole life," Sophy sighed. "It's the only meaningful sort of career they can imagine. Your defense of my plans gave me some creditability because you have credibility in their eyes. Knowing you respected my ideas made them think twice."

"Sophy . . ."

"I'm rather grateful, Max."

"I don't want your gratitude," he half snarled.

"I didn't think I'd ever have reason to be grateful to a professor of mathematics, but it just goes to show, you never can tell," she went on, sounding vaguely surprised.

"Consider it a dividend on your investment!"

Something told Sophy it might be time to shut up. Max's temper these days had grown somewhat unpredictable. A woman in love learned to read the signs, she told herself wisely.

And then she realized exactly what she'd said. A woman in love.

She was in love with Max Travers. In love with a wizard. How could it have happened? Two hours later, as she threw her magenta suitcases onto the bed and began to unpack, Sophy was still turning the question over in her mind.

Could she really be more than a pack of crayons for

Max Travers? Maybe the urge to play with them was simply a momentary diversion for him. But people like Max Travers, she reminded herself, rarely allowed themselves momentary diversions. They were too intent on the important things in life, like mathematics.

Max had been very silent tonight when he'd dropped her off at her apartment after the flight. He hadn't even attempted to kiss her good night. All he'd said as she got out of the car was that he'd see her at work in the morning. What had he been thinking? That he was tired of pursuing a pack of crayons who continually made life difficult for him? With a groan of apprehension and gloom, Sophy got undressed and went to bed.

For someone who had prided herself on her ability to deal with the real world, she seemed to have gotten herself into one heck of a mess.

It wasn't Max whom she saw first at work the next morning, however, it was Marcie Fremont. The other woman was already at work when Sophy entered the office. Marcie was always hard at work, Sophy thought with a rueful smile.

"How was the weekend?" Marcie poured coffee for both of them, eyeing Sophy curiously.

"Confusing. Interesting. Strange. I'm not sure how the weekend was, Marcie. My major accomplishment was surviving an academic reception without finding myself all alone in a corner."

"I can't imagine you ever finding yourself all alone in a corner at a party."

"I used to. Regularly. At least at academic parties. But it was different this time. It's been a while. I didn't realize how much I'd changed."

"A good feeling?"

"Yes." Sophy considered that further. "Yes, it was. I actually felt relaxed. Definitely a change for the better," she concluded firmly.

Two hours later the phone on Marcie's desk rang imperiously. Sophy, who had been just about to leave with her friend for coffee, paused and waited as Marcie picked up the receiver. And then intuition made her lunge forward to grab the instrument from her friend's hand before she had even spoken a greeting.

"S & J Technology, Miss Bennet speaking," Sophy said crisply, waving off Marcie. "Yes, this is Miss Fremont's office. She's busy at the moment. May I take a message? . . . Oh, I see. Well, perhaps I could slip a message into the conference room where she's conducting the meeting. Would you care to hold?" Regally Sophy put the call on hold and turned to an astonished Marcie.

"It's them! It's that company in California. The vice-president we contacted!"

Marcie's eyes widened as she reached for the phone. Sophy saw that her fingers trembled slightly.

"Oh, Sophy. This is it!"

"Not yet. You mustn't sound too eager. You're an executive they're trying to pirate away, remember? You're only vaguely interested in the position."

"Vaguely interested!" But Marcie dropped her hand and smiled reluctantly. "What now?"

"We let them wait on hold for a few minutes, and then you come to the phone, a bit irritable but aloofly polite."

"Oh, my God!"

"You can do it."

And Marcie did do it. Beautifully. When they finally rescued the unfortunate caller from several minutes on hold, Marcie was in perfect command of herself. Cool, in charge, full of executive presence. And when she eventually hung up the phone, she stared at Sophy with eyes that shone.

"They're begging me to come to work for them. I've

been offered my choice of two management positions. One reports directly to the president!"

"That's the one you'll take." Sophy grinned decisively. "We'll let them stew a couple of days and then you'll accept."

"And in the meantime?"

"In the meantime, we'll go have that coffee we were heading for when we were so rudely interrupted."

The two women walked to the elevators, drawing stares, as usual, because of the contrast they presented. They were unaware of the attention, however. Coffee break this morning was going to be a celebration.

Two days later Marcie made her phone call to California, and the excited, grateful company in California promised everything including a first-class airplane seat for the interview, which would be "merely a formality."

"You'll do beautifully," Sophy assured her, and then she reached for the phone on her own desk.

Max answered a bit brusquely and she knew she'd caught him in the middle of something. He softened immediately when he realized who was on the other end.

"I have to talk to you, Max," Sophy told him without preamble.

He didn't hesitate. "I'll be right down. The cafeteria?"

"Fine." She'd been spending a lot of time discussing business in the cafeteria lately, Sophy thought wryly.

Five minutes later she walked into the nearly empty room and found that Max had already obtained two cups of coffee and a private table. He looked up a bit warily as she came striding briskly toward him, and then his expression became impassive.

"It's over, Max." Sophy sat down and reached for her coffee. There was a deadly silence from the other side of the table. When she raised her eyes from her cup, she found Max looking at her with such intensity that she swallowed awkwardly and nearly choked.

"No."

That was all he said. She blinked in confusion. "But, Max, it is. There's nothing you can do. It's over."

"The hell it is!" He leaned forward, his palms flat on the table, eyes glittering icily behind the lenses of his glasses. "You're not going to just calmly phone me up and invite me for coffee and then tell me it's over. Not after all I've been through!"

Sophy edged back in her seat, shocked by the rough vehemence in his words. "Max, I'm sorry I started this whole thing by telling you what Marcie had planned, but at the time I sort of . . . well, panicked. I never wanted you to go to management with the information. But now everything's changed. Marcie has a new job and she'll be leaving the company soon. There's no way Graham Younger can ever implicate her in corporate espionage. You never even completed the phony model. There was no espionage."

"Marcie!" Max looked dumbfounded. "We're talking about Marcie? About your mysterious plans?"

"Well, of course. My plans to get Marcie a job in management. What did you think we were talking about?"

"You and me."

"Oh." Nonplussed, Sophy eyed him cautiously. He looked vastly relieved and at the same time thoroughly annoyed. "Well, uh, we're not. We're talking about the end of Younger's idiotic little scheme to trap Marcie and her 'web of conspirators.' Now we're going to have to tell Younger his brilliant plan didn't work, and I'm going to take great pleasure in doing so, if you want the truth."

She stood decisively and Max followed more reluctantly. "Uh . . . Sophy, there's something I have to tell you. You know this brilliant plan you've been criticizing from the beginning?" He ushered her into the elevator.

"What about it?"

"Well, it wasn't exactly Graham Younger's idea."

"Edison's? The head of Security?"

"Nope. It was all mine," he sighed.

"Yours!" Sophy stared up at him, her mouth falling open in astonishment. "It was *your* idea to play out this silly farce just for the sake of trapping poor Marcie Fremont? But, Max . . .!"

"I'm afraid so. Younger and Edison and I agreed before the meeting with you that you'd be more likely to go along with it if you thought it was a request from your boss. Besides, Younger thought it was a pretty good scheme. One that would work. He was willing enough to take credit for it."

"But, Max . . .!" She swallowed. "Why?"

"Not because I give a damn about Marcie Fremont and her potential as a corporate espionage agent, that's for sure!" The elevator doors slid open on the executive suite floor. "You can bet I normally don't get involved in such mundane things as corporate security," he growled.

"So why did you become involved?"

"The single merit of this asinine scheme was that it ensured that you had to keep seeing me. Think about it."

"But, Max," Sophy couldn't help but say, "it was such a silly idea."

"I know. You'd think I'd have enough sense to stick to mathematics, wouldn't you?"

11

"You were marvelously arrogant with Younger and Edison, Max." Sophy gave him a mischievous smile as she sat across from him at dinner that night. "Thanks."

The scene in Graham Younger's office had not been pleasant, Max reflected as he munched the taco salad Sophy had insisted he sample. Younger and Edison were both angry at having had their potential prey snatched from their grasp.

They had been even more furious to learn they'd been outmaneuvered by a mere secretary. And word of Marcie's new management position had made Younger positively livid, especially when Sophy explained just how much Marcie's undervalued knowledge of S & J's Quality Control would benefit her new employer.

Sophy had seemed rather unconcerned about her boss's attempt to make mincemeat out of her, although Max had caught a flash of appreciative gratitude in her eyes when he'd stepped in and restored a certain civility to the proceedings.

And now she was thanking him. No, she wasn't actually *thanking* him, Max decided unhappily, she was merely complimenting him on having put the other two men in their place. She hadn't really needed him to defend her, he realized. Sophy didn't seem to *need* him for anything.

Therein lay the crux of his whole problem.

Max picked up his wine. "You were a little arrogant yourself."

She shrugged, the frilly, flounced sleeve of her red dinner dress shifting intriguingly. "I can afford to be a bit uppity." She grinned. "I'll be quitting soon."

"To open your boutique?"

"Ummm. How do you like the taco salad, Max?"

"I'm not sure I like hamburger and corn chips in my salads."

"You'll get used to it."

"I doubt it. I'm going back to North Carolina on Wednesday." He delivered the statement with a deliberate lack of intonation. How would she react? Probably be thrilled.

There was a beat of hesitation, and for the life of him he couldn't begin to imagine what she was thinking. "Where you can eat hush puppies all day long and work on math equations? Are you sure you can readapt? What about that Texas drawl you're working on?"

Max was suddenly tired of the flippancy. "Why don't you come back with me and find out what happens to it?"

Sophy flushed. "Sorry. I keep my visits to Chapel Hill to a minimum. I love my parents, but I knew a long time ago I couldn't live too close to them or spend too much time with them. I don't have to be in their company five minutes before they're giving such useful advice as telling me to go back for my master's."

"They aren't fighting your boutique idea," he
178

pointed out carefully. She was avoiding the point, but he let her for the moment.

"Only because you defended it. People back down when you come to the rescue. Have you noticed that, Max? Younger, Edison, my parents, poor Nick. They all either respect your opinion or are intimidated by you now. Quite a track record."

"Except you."

"Except me. Would you like me to be intimidated by you, Max?"

"No. I'd like you to need me," he said flatly. She went very still. "The way I need you."

"Max," Sophy said. "You don't need me. Not really. I don't fit in your world. I never have. You'd be bored with me in two months!"

"Come back with me for two months and find out."

"No!"

"I think the truth of the matter is that you're the one who's afraid she'll be bored. Bored with a staid, sober, dull professor of mathematics." He looked straight into her eyes. "Sophy, I've given this a lot of thought. The only way things will ever really work between us is if you discover on some level that you need me. You have to decide that you really need me in your life." He spoke slowly, setting everything out in the open. He had nothing left to lose. "And there may come a time when you do decide that, Sophy."

"Max, I don't know what you're trying to say, but . . ."

"But I think you need a little time. You're basically a very bright young woman, just as your parents have claimed all along," he noted whimsically. "And now I believe you need some time to think."

"About what, Dr. Travers?"

"About such matters as why I kept wanting to see you, be with you, whenever possible, even though you

179

had sworn you wouldn't go to bed with me again. About why I stepped outside my area of expertise to concoct that ridiculous scheme and then convinced Graham Younger to involve you in it. About a lot of things."

"Oh, Max . . .!" she wailed softly. "I don't know. I can't seem to think. It's all so confusing."

"That's why I'm going back to North Carolina on Wednesday. Sophy, when you've thought it all out and made your decision, I'll be waiting." He leaned forward to catch her agitated fingers and squeeze them gently. "Come back to Chapel Hill anytime, sweetheart. You'll find me there, waiting for you."

Max sat in his third-floor corner office, oblivious to the lush green grounds of the campus outside his window, and wondered if he was going out of his mind.

He hadn't been able to concentrate on anything since he had returned from Dallas. Oh, he'd gotten through the work on his desk and occasionally he'd picked up an article in one of the many esoteric journals he read. But the intense concentration that had always characterized him seemed to have disappeared. He had to struggle to think of anything at all except Sophy.

It had only been five days since he'd left Dallas. Monday morning. He had a graduate seminar in half an hour. He hoped he could fake his way through it. Shouldn't be too difficult. The students were studying the work of Evariste Galois, the brilliant French mathematician who, because of his fiery temper, had managed to get himself killed in a duel at the age of twenty. People had wondered for years just how much Galois might have gone on to contribute to the world of mathematics if his temper hadn't been quite so passionate. Before his death he had already established himself as one of the most original thinkers who ever lived.

For the first time in his life Max thought he understood Evariste Galois. Never before had he been able to comprehend a man as brilliant as Galois letting himself get sidetracked from his real work long enough to become involved in such an idiotic thing as a duel over a woman. Now he could.

He'd skip the graduate seminar altogether if it meant he could fight another cowboy for Sophy. Some things were more important than math.

He *must* be going out of his mind to think that!

Max crumpled the piece of paper he'd idly been twisting into a Möbius strip, a shape with the curious property of having only one side, and listened to the staccato tap of a pair of high heels out in the hall.

The sound reminded him of Sophy. Bright, energetic, alive. He wondered who on the third floor had worn high heels today. Usually the women in his department wore more sensible shoes.

The aggressive tap of the heels came to a halt outside his door and he glanced up automatically, aware that his body was tense with anticipation, just because of the sound of a pair of high heels that reminded him of Sophy. Things were getting worse. He really was going to go slowly out of his mind if he didn't do something drastic.

The knock on the door made him frown. "Come in." Simultaneously he realized that the sound of the high heels in the corridor had stopped. Whoever was knocking on his door was wearing the shoes. It was going to be painful to have the door open and find another woman besides Sophy standing there.

But the door opened and it wasn't another woman. "Sophy!" Max surged to his feet. He felt dazed. "Sophy," he repeated far more softly. He realized he was staring, but he couldn't help himself. It was almost impossible to believe she was here in his office, bringing light and color and confusion to his orderly surroundings. Her mane of curls seemed more delightfully frizzy than ever. The high heels he had heard tapping out the exciting rhythm in the hall were purple. Max thought vaguely that he'd never seen purple shoes. They went wonderfully with the purple and red dress she was wearing. Nobody else he knew could successfully wear purple and red. But the best color of all was the strange blue-green shade of her eyes. And right now those eyes were smiling at him.

"Hello, Max," she said softly. "I brought you something." She came toward him, carrying a small package in her right hand.

Feeling as if he were moving under the force of a spell, Max extended his hand for the gift. It wasn't what he wanted to do. What he really wanted to do was grab Sophy and hold her close to make certain she was real and not a bright illusion. She put the package in his fingers and he looked down at it.

"Sophy." He wasn't certain what to say next, so he tried to concentrate on unwrapping the package. The paper fell away beneath his unusually clumsy attempts, and he stared at the box of crayons, a slow smile edging the corner of his mouth. "Thank you." Damn it, couldn't he think of anything more intelligent?

"Do you still want me, Max?"

He heard the uncertainty and the wistful hope in her voice and groaned, dropping the crayons on his desk to walk around the front and pull her into his arms. "Sophy, honey, I've been sitting here for five days thinking about what I was going to do if you didn't come to me." He buried his face in the cascading curls and inhaled deeply. "My God, Sophy, I can't believe you're really here."

He held her close, and when her arms went around his waist he muttered her name again and searched out her mouth. For a long moment they clung together, mouths joined in heated dampness, their bodies touching intimately. Max let the tension seep out of his body, felt the happiness welling up inside. She was here. He couldn't believe his luck.

"Sophy, honey, I know I'm no macho cowboy . . ."

"No," she laughed into his shirt, "you're a macho university professor. Until you came along, I didn't know they existed. You've got a foot in both worlds now."

"So do you. How can you doubt it after the way you handled yourself at that faculty reception? And the way you handle yourself in the corporate world is a bit frightening! Someday I want to hear the whole story of how you got Marcie Fremont that job in California."

"Someday I'll tell you. You'll probably be shocked, though."

"Nothing you can do would shock me anymore," he murmured.

"Then maybe you really have come out of your ivory tower!" She lifted her head abruptly. "What would you have done, Max, if I hadn't come to Chapel Hill?" she asked, her eyes wide and inviting.

"I told myself I'd give you a month or so and then I'd find some excuse to fly back to Dallas. I was making lists of reasons I could give S & J Technology for having to update that math model I did for them."

"Your creativity outside the realm of math leaves me breathless," Sophy laughed gently.

"Don't worry. When creativity fails me I can always fall back on my new macho mentality."

"The direct approach?"

"Umm. Like carrying you off over my shoulder."

"Max, you wouldn't! Imagine what your colleagues would think."

"That's their problem. I learned a few things down in Texas."

"Yes, I know." Sophy grinned ruefully. "Like how to fix plumbing, and grill steaks, and wear stylish ties." She let her hand trail lightly down his shoulder to the tie he was wearing. She smoothed it affectionately. "You're going to wear out your new tie, Max."

"You can make me another one."

"I will."

"A wedding gift?" he suggested tenderly.

"You want to marry me?" He saw the flutter of hope and joy in her eyes and gathered her close again.

"That's the logical conclusion when two people are in love."

"Love? You love me, Max? Are you sure?"

"I'm very, very sure." He wrapped her close, his voice husky and low. "Only love could have made me go crazy that night after you discovered that dumb cowboy was cheating on you. I've never taken advantage of a woman before in my life! A whole lifetime of being a gentleman went up in smoke. And the worst part was that I didn't regret it afterward. That was just the beginning. When I found myself concocting ridiculous schemes so that I could have an excuse to go on seeing you, I knew I was in over my head."

"Oh, Max, I've always been so careful to steer clear of people in your world. I was intimidated by wizards for so long. I couldn't bear the thought of loving a man who couldn't possibly respect me as an equal."

"Sophy, you have your own kind of wizardry. You're an artist and a businesswoman. Do you realize what a rare combination that is? Few people have the ability to be both. I have a tremendous respect for your abilities."

"But my parents always thought—"

"Darling, I'm very fond of your parents. They've been wonderful to me. But I'm aware they're a little blind where you're concerned. They love you deeply, but they don't quite understand you. That's why they've always tried to push you back into their world— a world they do understand."

Sophy slanted a wondering glance at his loving eyes.

"You're a bridge between my world and theirs, aren't you, Max?"

He gave her a strange half smile and shook his head. "No, you're the bridge, Sophy. For all of us. If it wasn't for you in their lives, occasionally turning it upside down and filling it with confusion, your mother and father undoubtedly would have turned out a lot like my parents. Cold and unemotional and completely secluded in their academic world. I probably would have wound up like my parents, too, if it hadn't been for you. I was well on my way! But I looked out of my ivory tower one day and saw what I'd been missing."

"The fun of brawling with cowboys?" she taunted gently.

"And the joy of eating popcorn while watching old sci-fi flicks, and of seducing you. Most of all seducing you. I need you. You make my life complete. But I can't help wondering why you love me, although I'm not about to question my luck!"

She saw the anxious hope in his eyes and lifted her fingers to smooth the harsh brackets around his mouth. "Much to my astonishment, I found myself loving you for some of the same reasons you say you love me," she admitted softly. "When you left Dallas all the color went out of my life. But it's so much more than that. I realized I had to take the chance of going to you. Our worlds may be different, but they complement each other. You make me feel complete. I love you."

He was watching her face with raw hunger now in his eyes. There was a longing in him that was a combination of love and desire and need, and Sophy felt herself responding to the potent mixture.

"I never thought wizards were capable of real passion for anything except their work until I met you," she breathed.

"You bring out the passionate side of me, along with a few other sides I didn't know existed."

"And you bring out some sides of me I didn't know existed, either. I've taken risks with you I've never even thought of taking with any other man. I can't imagine being willing to come back to Chapel Hill for any other man. But with you I was willing to take the chance. And I can't imagine letting myself get seduced by a man I hardly even knew the way I did with you. Oh, Max, we've both done some crazy things around each other, haven't we?"

"We should have realized it was love right from the beginning," he drawled.

"But I thought I had nothing worthwhile to give a wizard," she said wistfully.

"And I thought I had nothing worthwhile to offer someone like you, who seemed to have everything and who seemed to prefer cowboys. Sophy, will you marry me and live with me for the rest of our lives?"

She linked her arms around his neck and smiled dreamily. "Yes," she whispered, touching her lips to his. "Yes, yes, yes." A teasing light came into her eyes. "But do you suppose North Carolina is ready for my style of clothing design?"

She felt Max's warm chuckle as it moved through his chest. "Possibly not. But even if it is, I'm rather inclined to agree with your feeling that you should live some distance from your parents. It's true that you now have me to run interference with them when they start worrying overmuch about your lifestyle, but I think, all things considered, we'd be better off in Texas."

"Texas!" Startled, she stared up at him. He ruffled the curling halo of her hair and smiled.

"Umm. I hate to sound arrogant about this, knowing as I do how you feel about arrogant math wizards, but frankly, I can write my own ticket to any school in the country. How does Austin sound? I know it's not Dallas, but . . ."

"Austin. You're going to get a job at the University of Texas?"

"Why not? I had an offer from them last year, which I put on ice as I usually do. But if I were to change my mind, I don't think there would be any problem."

"But, Max, you've got tenure here."

"Tenure isn't particularly important to me. Your career is a lot more important. And I think you could pursue it better in a wide-open state like Texas than you could in North Carolina. And in Texas you won't have to worry about your charming parents gazing over your shoulder all the time."

"You really mean that, don't you? You're willing to take another position in another state for my sake? Max, I don't know what to say. I'm stunned."

"The expression is very becoming on you. Don't worry, honey, it's all going to work out perfectly."

"But will you be happy in Texas?"

"Sweetheart, I've begun to think lately that I was born in Texas," he drawled in his new accent. "I fit right in down there. Didn't you notice? I spent all my spare time brawling and grilling steaks and taking you to bed. A classic Texan. First thing I'm going to do when we get there is buy a pair of hand-tooled cowboy boots suitable for squashing rattlesnakes."

"Max, I love you."

"I love you." He feathered her mouth lightly with his own and then suddenly remembered something.

"Sweetheart, I'm supposed to be teaching a graduate seminar in about two minutes . . ."

She noticed that he didn't sound too concerned. "Really?"

"But I think my students will understand that mathematics can't always come first," he murmured, reaching behind him to punch an intercom button. Quickly, he arranged for an associate to take his place, then beckoned her. "Right now I've got other things on my mind besides teaching class. We Texans keep our priorities straight, you know."

"Ah, the marvelous, multidimensional, eminently logical mind of a wizard," she murmured, going back into his arms. "As a matter of fact, I was thinking about keeping the same priorities straight."

"Must be a case of great minds traveling on the same path."

"Could be. You know, I've come to the conclusion you're going to be very useful around the house, Max. I've got this checkbook that hasn't been balanced in six months, for starters."

"It's so nice to feel needed." He grinned wickedly. "Honey, I will be happy to barbecue your meals, fix your plumbing, fight off cowboys and balance your checkbook. But there is a price for a wizard's services. I believe I once pointed out that I don't come cheap."

"What's the price?"

"Let me show you." His mouth came down on hers, and Sophy gave herself up to the wizardry of love.

ENTER:

Here's your chance to win a fabulous $50,000 diamond jewelry collection, consisting of diamond necklace, bracelet, earrings and ring.

All you have to do to enter is fill out the coupon below and mail it by September 30, 1985.

Send entries to:

In the U.S. Silhouette Diamond Sweepstakes
P.O. Box 779
Madison Square Station
New York, NY 10159

In Canada Silhouette Diamond Sweepstakes
Suite 191
238 Davenport Road
Toronto, Ontario M5R 1J6

NAME_____

ADDRESS_____

CITY_____STATE/(PROV.)_____

ZIP/(POSTAL CODE)_____

BCD-A-1

RULES FOR SILHOUETTE DIAMOND SWEEPSTAKES

OFFICIAL RULES—NO PURCHASE NECESSARY

1. Silhouette Diamond Sweepstakes is open to Canadian (except Quebec) and United States residents 18 years or older at the time of entry. Employees and immediate families of the publishers of Silhouette, their affiliates, retailers, distributors, printers, agencies and RONALD SMILEY INC. are excluded.

2. To enter, print your name and address on the official entry form or on a 3" x 5" slip of paper. You may enter as often as you choose, but each envelope must contain only one entry. Mail entries first class in Canada to Silhouette Diamond Sweepstakes, Suite 191, 238 Davenport Road, Toronto, Ontario M5R 1J6. In the United States, mail to Silhouette Diamond Sweepstakes, P.O. Box 779, Madison Square Station, New York, NY 10159. Entries must be postmarked between February 1 and September 30, 1985. Silhouette is not responsible for lost, late or misdirected mail.

3. First Prize of diamond jewelry, consisting of a necklace, ring, bracelet and earrings will be awarded. Approximate retail value is $50,000 U.S./$62,500 Canadian. Second Prize of 100 Silhouette Home Reader Service Subscriptions will be awarded. Approximate retail value of each is $162.00 U.S./$180.00 Canadian. No substitution, duplication, cash redemption or transfer of prizes will be permitted. Odds of winning depend upon the number of valid entries received. One prize to a family or household. Income taxes, other taxes and insurance on First Prize are the sole responsibility of the winners.

4. Winners will be selected under the supervision of RONALD SMILEY INC., an independent judging organization whose decisions are final, by random drawings from valid entries postmarked by September 30, 1985, and received no later than October 7, 1985. Entry in this sweepstakes indicates your awareness of the Official Rules. Winners who are residents of Canada must answer correctly a time-related arithmetical skill-testing question to qualify. First Prize winner will be notified by certified mail and must submit an Affidavit of Compliance within 10 days of notification. Returned Affidavits or prizes that are refused or undeliverable will result in alternative names being randomly drawn. Winners may be asked for use of their name and photo at no additional compensation.

5. For a First Prize winner list, send a stamped self-addressed envelope postmarked by September 30, 1985. In Canada, mail to Silhouette Diamond Contest Winner, Suite 309, 238 Davenport Road, Toronto, Ontario M5R 1J6. In the United States, mail to Silhouette Diamond Contest Winner, P.O. Box 182, Bowling Green Station, New York, NY 10274. This offer will appear in Silhouette publications and at participating retailers. Offer void in Quebec and subject to all Federal, Provincial, State and Municipal laws and regulations and wherever prohibited or restricted by law.

SDR-A-1

READERS' COMMENTS ON SILHOUETTE DESIRES

"Thank you for Silhouette Desires. They are the best thing that has happened to the bookshelves in a long time."
— V.W.*, Knoxville, TN

"Silhouette Desires—wonderful, fantastic—the best romance around."
— H.T.*, Margate, N.J.

"As a writer as well as a reader of romantic fiction, I found DESIREs most refreshingly realistic—and definitely as magical as the love captured on their pages."
— C.M.*, Silver Lake, N.Y.

"I just wanted to let you know how very much I enjoy your Silhouette Desire books. I read other romances, and I must say your books rate up at the top of the list."
— C.N.*, Anaheim, CA

"Desires are number one. I especially enjoy the endings because they just don't leave you with a kiss or embrace; they finish the story. Thank you for giving me such reading pleasure."
— M.S.*, Sandford, FL

*names available on request